EMMAUS

EMMAUS

ALESSANDRO BARICCO

translated by
ANN GOLDSTEIN

McSWEENEY'S BOOKS
SAN FRANCISCO

www.mcsweeneys.net

Printed in Michigan by Thomson-Shore

McSweeney's and colophon are registered trademarks of McSweeney's,
a privately held company with wildly fluctuating resources.

ISBN: 978-1936365-59-3

To Dario Voltini and Davide Longo

The red sports car made a U-turn and pulled over in front of the boy. The man in the driver's seat maneuvered calmly; he seemed to be in no hurry, to have no thoughts. He wore a stylish cap, the car's top was down. He stopped, and with a graceful smile said to the boy, Have you seen Andre?

Andre was a girl.

The boy misunderstood, he thought the man wanted to know if he had seen her in general, in life—if he had seen how marvelous she was. Have you *seen* Andre? Like a thing between men.

So the boy said yes.

Where? the man asked.

Given that the man continued to smile, in a way, the boy continued to misunderstand the questions. So he answered, Everywhere. Then it occurred to him to be more precise, and he added, From a distance.

The man then nodded, as if to say that he agreed, and that he had understood. He was still smiling. You're a smart kid, he said. And he pulled away, but without revving the engine—as if he had never had to rev up the engine in his life.

Four intersections farther on, where a signal flashed uselessly in the sun, the red sports car was hit by an out-of-control van.

It should be said that the man was Andre's father.

The boy was me.

It was many years ago.

His suffering was tremendous,
As tremendous as his love.

—Giovanni Battista Ferrandini,
The Virgin's Lament

EMMAUS

We're all sixteen or seventeen years old, but we aren't really aware of it: it's the only age we can imagine; we scarcely know the past. We're very normal, there is no plan for us except to be normal, it's something we've inherited in our blood. For generations, our families have worked to hone life to the point where every bit of evidence is removed—any rough spot that could get the attention of a distant eye. They ended up, in time, with a certain expertise in the field, masters of invisibility: the sure hand, the knowing eye—artisans. It's a world where you turn off the lights when you leave a room; the living room chairs are covered with plastic. Some elevators have a mechanism whereby if you insert a coin you gain the privilege of assisted ascent. Going down they are free, though in general considered unnecessary. Egg whites are saved in a glass in the refrigerator; we seldom go to restaurants, and then only on Sunday. On the balconies, tough, silent plants promising nothing are protected by green awnings from the dust of the streets. Light is often considered a disturbance. Grateful to the fog, absurd as it may seem, we live, if that is living.

Yet we are happy, or at least we think we are.

The apparatus of standard normality includes, incontrovertibly, the fact that we are Catholics—believers and Catholics. In reality it's the anomaly, the madness that overturns the theory of our simplicity, but to us it all seems very ordinary, regular. We believe, and there doesn't seem to be any other possibility. Yet we believe fiercely, hungrily; our faith is not tranquil but an uncontrolled passion, like a physical need, an urgency. It's the seed of some insanity—the obvious gathering of a storm on the horizon. But our fathers and mothers don't read the arriving tempest, seeing instead only a meek acquiescence in the family's course: and they let us put out to sea. Boys who spend their free time changing the sheets of sick people abandoned in their own shit: this is not taken by anyone for what it is—a form of madness. Or the taste for poverty, the pride in cast-off clothes. The prayers, the praying. The sense of guilt, always. We are misfits, but no one realizes it. We believe in the God of the Gospels.

So for us the world has physical confines that are very immediate, and mental confines as fixed as a liturgy. And that is our infinite.

In the distance, beyond the habitual, in a hyperspace we know almost nothing about, there are others, figures on the horizon. What's immediately noticeable is that they do not believe—apparently, they do not believe in anything—but also evident is a familiarity with money, and the sparkling reflections of their objects and their actions: the light. Probably they're just rich, and our gaze is the upward gaze of every bourgeoisie engaged in the effort of ascent—a gaze from the shadows. I don't know. But it's clear to us that in them, fathers and sons, the chemistry of life produces not precise formulas but, as if forgetful of its regulatory function, spectacular arabesques—drunken science. The result is lives that we don't understand—writings to which the key is lost. They are not moral, they are not prudent, they have no shame, and they've been that way for a very long time. Evidently they can count on improbably full granaries, because they squander the harvest of the seasons, whether it is money or even just knowledge, experience. They reap good and evil indifferently. They burn memory, and in the ashes read their future.

They're grand, and they go unpunished.

At a distance, they pass before our eyes, and sometimes through our thoughts. It can also happen that life, with its fluid daily adjustments, leads us to touch them, by chance, suspending for a brief moment the natural differences. Usually it's the parents who mingle—occasionally one of us, a passing friendship, a girl. So we can see them close up. When we return to the ranks—not expelled, really, but, rather, relieved of a burden—a few open pages, written in their language, linger in memory. The full, round sound that their fathers' racquet strings make when they hit the tennis ball. The houses, especially the ones at the sea or in the mountains, which they often seem to forget about: unhesitatingly they give the keys to their children; on the tables are dusty whiskey glasses, and in the corners antique sculptures, as in a museum, but patent-leather shoes stick out of the closets. The sheets: black. In the photographs: suntanned. When we study with them—at their houses—the telephone rings constantly and we see the mothers, who are often apologizing, but always with a laugh, and in a tone of voice that we don't recognize. Then they come over and run a hand through our hair, saying something girlish and pressing their breast against our arm. There are servants, too, and careless, seemingly improvised schedules—they don't seem to believe in the redeeming power of habit. They don't seem to believe in anything.

It's a world, and Andre comes from it. Remote, she appears from time to time, always in matters that have nothing to do with us. Although she's our age, she mostly hangs around with older people, and this makes her even more alien. We see her—it's hard to say if she ever sees us. Probably she doesn't even know our names. Hers is Andrea: in our families it's a boys' name, but not in hers, which even when it comes to names demonstrates an instinctive inclination to privilege. Nor did the family stop there, because they call her Andre, with the accent on the *A*; it's a name that exists only for her. So she has always been, for everyone, Andre. She is, of course, very pretty, most of them are, over there, but it should be said that she is pretty in a particular way, unintentional. There's something masculine about her. A hardness. This makes things easier for us. We are Catholics: beauty is a moral virtue, and the body has nothing to do with it, so the curve of a behind means nothing, the perfect turn of a slender ankle means nothing: the female body is the object of a systematic deferment. In short, all we know of our inevitable heterosexuality we've learned from the dark eyes of a best friend or the lips of a companion we were jealous of. The skin, every so often, with faint movements that we don't understand, under the soccer shirts. So it goes without saying that slightly masculine girls are more attractive to us. In this, Andre is perfect. She wears her hair long, but with the frenzy of an American Indian—you never see her fix or brush it, it's just there. All her wonder is in her face—the color of her eyes, the angle of her cheekbones, her mouth. It seems unnecessary to look elsewhere: her body is just a way of standing, resting her weight, walking away—it's a consequence. None of us ever wondered what she's like under the sweater, it's not urgent for us to know, and we're grateful. Her way of moving, at every instant, is enough—an inherited elegance of gestures and low voices, an extension of her beauty. At our age none of us really control our body, we walk with the hesitation of a colt, we have voices not our own: but she appears old, knowing the nuances of every state of being, by instinct. It's clear that the other girls try the same moves and intonations, but they seldom succeed, because what in her is a gift—grace—in them is a construct. In dressing as in being—at every instant.

So, from a distance, we are enchanted, as, it must be said, are others, everyone. The older boys know her beauty, and even older men, of forty. Her friends know it, and all the mothers—hers, too, like a wound in her side. They all know that that's how it is, and that nothing can be done about it.

As far as we understand, there's no one who can say he's been Andre's boyfriend. We've never seen her holding hands. Or a kiss—not even just a light touch on a boy's skin. It isn't her style. She doesn't care about being liked by *someone*—she seems involved in something else, more complicated. There are boys who should attract her, very different from us, obviously, like her brother's friends, who dress well, and speak with a strange accent, as if it were important to move their lips as little as possible. There might also be adult males around who to us seem revolting. Men with cars. And in fact it happens that you see Andre go off with them—in their revolting cars or on motorcycles. Especially at night—as if the darkness carried her into a cone of shadow that we don't want to understand. But all this has nothing to do with the natural flow of things—of boys and girls together. It's like a sequence from which certain passages have been removed. It doesn't result in what we call love.

So Andre belongs to no one—but we know that she also belongs to everyone. It could be part of the legend, certainly, but the stories are rich in details, as if someone had seen, and knows. And we *recognize* her, in those stories—it's difficult for us to visualize the rest, but she, there in the midst, really is herself. Her way of doing things. She waits in the bathroom at the movie theater, leaning against a wall, and they go in one after the other to take her: she doesn't even turn around. Then she leaves, without going back to the theater to get her coat. They go whoring with her, and she laughs a lot, standing in a corner, watching—if they are transvestites, she looks at them and touches them. She never drinks, she doesn't smoke, she fucks lucidly, knowing what she's doing, and, it's said, always in silence. There are some Polaroids around, which we've never seen, where she is the only woman. She doesn't care about being photographed, doesn't care that sometimes it's the fathers, after the sons; she doesn't seem to care about anything. Every morning, again, she belongs to no one.

It's hard for us to understand. In the afternoon we go to the hospital, the one for poor people. Men's ward, urology. Under the covers the sick men don't wear pajama bottoms but have a rubber tube inserted in their urethra. That tube is connected to another, slightly bigger tube, which empties into a transparent plastic bag, attached to the side of the bed. That's how the sick men pee; they're not even aware of it, and they don't have to get up. Everything ends up in the transparent bag; the urine is watery, or dark, as red as blood. What we do is empty those damn bags. You have to disconnect the two tubes, detach the bag, go to the bathroom carrying that full bladder, and empty it into the toilet. Then we return to the ward and put everything back in place. The hard part is the business of disconnecting—with your fingers you squeeze the tube that's inserted in the urethra, and then you have to give it a tug, otherwise it doesn't slip out of the other tube, the one for the bag, but you try to do it gently. We talk while we're doing it—we say something to the sick people, something cheerful, as we bend over them, trying not to hurt them. They could care less at that moment about our questions, because all they're thinking about is that gunshot in their dick, but they answer, between their teeth, because they know that we're doing it for them, the talking. You empty the bag by pulling out a red plug in the lower corner. Often there are urinary sands on the bottom, like the dregs in a bottle. So you have to wash it thoroughly. We do this because we believe in the God of the Gospels.

As for Andre, it should be said that one time we saw her with our own eyes, in a bar—at a certain time of night, leather sofas and low lights, with a lot of those other people. We were there by mistake, because we wanted a sandwich at that time of night. Andre was sitting with others, with those people. She got up and went outside, passing close by us—she leaned against the hood of a sports car, double-parked, with its hazards on. One of those people arrived and opened the car doors, and they both got in. We were eating our sandwiches, standing up. They didn't move from there—it must not have mattered much that cars passed by, and even a few people on foot. She leaned over, putting her head between the wheel and the boy's chest: he was laughing, meanwhile, and looking straight ahead. The door concealed everything, obviously, but every so often you could see her head through the window: she raised it and glanced outside, according to a rhythm of her own. One of those times he put his hand on her head to push it down again, but Andre shoved the hand away with an angry gesture—and yelled something. We went on eating our sandwiches, as if spellbound. They remained in that ridiculous position for a while, without talking—Andre seemed like a turtle with its head sticking out. But then she lowered her head again, down, behind the door. The boy leaned back. We finished our sandwiches, and finally the boy got out of the car, laughed, and adjusted his jacket so that it hung straight. They went back into the bar. Andre passed by and looked at one of us as if she were trying to remember something. Then she went in and sat down again on the leather sofa.

That was a real blow job, said Bobby, who knew what it was—the only one of us who knew, exactly, what a blow job was. He had had a girlfriend who did it. So he confirmed that it was a blow job, no doubt about it. We continued to walk in silence, and it was clear that each of us was trying to put things together, to imagine in detail what had happened behind the car door. We were making a mental image, focusing on the foreground. We worked with the little we had: I had saved up merely a glimpse of my girlfriend with the tip of my dick in her mouth, but just barely—she held it there, not moving, her eyes strangely wide, a little too wide. From there to imagining Andre—it wasn't so simple, of course. But it must have been easier for Bobby, certainly, and maybe even for Luca, who is reserved about such things but must have seen and done more than I have. As for the Saint, he is different. I don't want to talk about him—not now. And anyway he is someone who, in thinking about what to do when he grows up, does not exclude the priesthood. He doesn't say it, but you understand. He's the one who found the work at the hospital—it's one of the things we do in our free time. Before, we used to go and visit old people in their tiny houses—they were poor, forgotten old people and we brought them food. Then the Saint discovered that business of the poor people's hospital, and he said that it would be great. In fact, we like going out into the air afterward, with the odor of pee still in our nostrils; we walk with pride. Under the covers, the penises of the sick old men are tired, and the hair around them is all white, white like their heads. They're very poor, and don't have relatives to bring them a newspaper; their mouths are putrid; they complain in a nauseating way. There's a lot of disgust to overcome, because of the filth, the smells, and the details of the job; yet we are able to do it, and in exchange we get something we wouldn't know how to explain—a kind of certainty, the rocklike substance of a certainty. So we go out into the darkness more solid, and apparently more true. It's the same darkness that every evening swallows up Andre and her lost adventures, in those other latitudes of life: arctic, extreme. Odd though it may seem, there is a single darkness, for all.

One of us, as you've seen, is called Bobby. He has an older brother who looks just like John F. Kennedy. So he's Bobby.

One night, his mother was putting things away in the kitchen—they ended up talking about Andre. Our mothers talk about Andre, if the subject comes up, while our fathers pull back, with an indecipherable grimace: she's so beautiful and scandalous it embarrasses them to talk about her—they want to be seen as asexual. So Bobby's mother talked about her, with him. She said, Poor girl. Poor girl wasn't what came to Bobby's mind, if he thought about Andre. So his mother had to explain. She rolled the napkins and put them in the rings, not wood but colored plastic. She said that that girl was not like others. I know, Bobby said. No, you don't know, she said. And then she added that Andre had killed herself— it had happened some time ago. They were silent for a bit. Bobby's mother didn't know if it was right to go on. She tried to kill herself, she said, finally. Then she begged Bobby not to say a word to anyone—that's how we got to know.

She had chosen a rainy day. She was wearing a lot of clothes. Under everything she had put on a pair of her brother's underpants. Then she had continued with T-shirts, sweaters, and a skirt over pants. Also gloves. A hat and two coats, a lighter one, and then a heavy one on top. She had put on rubber boots—green rubber boots. Like that she had left, and gone to the bridge over the river. Since it was night, no one was there. A few cars, unwilling to stop. Andre had started walking in the rain; what she wanted was to get completely soaked and become as heavy as a piece of wreckage. She walked for a long time, back and forth, until she felt the weight of all that sopping-wet stuff. Then she climbed up on the iron railing and jumped into the water, which at that hour was black—the water of the black river.

Someone saved her.

But those who begin to die never stop, and now we know why Andre attracts us beyond any common sense, and in spite of our every conviction. We see her laugh, or do things like ride on a motor scooter, and pat a dog—some afternoons she goes around with a girlfriend, holding her by the hand, and she has a purse that she puts useful things in. Yet we no longer believe in it, because we're thinking of how she suddenly turns her head, eyes terrified, searching for something—oxygen. Even the habit she has—her neck bent back, chin raised—the habit of standing like that. On the invisible surface of the water. And each of her disappearances, including those which are unmentionable and shameless, which we don't know how to describe. They're like flashes, and we understand them.

It's that she's dying. Andre—dying.

Then Bobby asked his mother why Andre had done it, but his mother got a little difficult there, he guessed that she didn't really want to tell the rest of the story, she closed a drawer suddenly, with more force than necessary: our mothers waste nothing, not even the pressure of a wrist on a drawer handle—but she did it, and that was to say that she wasn't going to talk about it anymore.

Once we went to the bridge, at night, because we wanted to see the black water—*that* black water. Me, Bobby, the Saint, and Luca, who is my best friend. We went on our bicycles, we wanted to see what Andre's eyes had seen, so to speak. And how high the air really was, if we were to consider jumping it. We also had half an idea of climbing up on the railing, or maybe leaning forward a little, over the void. Holding on tight, though, because we are all boys who get home in time for dinner—our families believe in routines and schedules. So we went: but the water was so black it seemed thick and heavy—mud, oil. It was horrible, and there was nothing else to say. We looked down, leaning on the icy iron of the railing, staring at the fat veins of the current, and the bottomless black.

If there was a force that could compel you to jump, we weren't acquainted with it. We are full of words whose true meaning we haven't been taught, and one of those words is *suffering*. Another is the word *death*. We don't know what they mean, but we use them, and this is a mystery. It also happens with less solemn words. Bobby once told me that when he was young, fourteen, he happened to go to a meeting at the church devoted to the subject of masturbation, and the odd thing was that he, at the time, didn't in fact know the meaning of the word *masturbation*—the truth was that he didn't understand what it was. But he had gone, and had said his bit and had a lively discussion, this he remembered well. He said that, thinking back, he wasn't even sure that *the others* knew what they were talking about. Possible that the only one there who actually jerked off was the priest, he said. Then, as he was telling this story, a doubt must have crossed his mind, and so he added, You know what I'm talking about, right?

Yes, I know. Masturbation, I know what it is.

Well, I didn't know, he said. I had in mind certain times when I rubbed against a pillow, at night, because I couldn't sleep. I put it between my legs and rubbed against it. Just that. And I had a discussion about it, that stuff, can you imagine?

But we're like that, we use a lot of words whose meaning we don't know, and one of those words is *suffering*. Another is the word *death*. That's why it wasn't possible for us to have Andre's eyes, and see the black water, from the bridge, as she had seen it. She who comes, rather, from a world without caution, in which the human adventure isn't protected by normality, but veers widely, until it touches the edge of every distant word, no matter how sharp—and first of all the one that means death. In their families, they often die without waiting for old age, as if impatient, and so familiar is the word *death* that not infrequently their recent past includes

the case of an uncle, a sister, a cousin who was killed—or who
has killed. We die, every so often; they are murderers and
murdered. If I try to explain the rift in caste that separates
us from them, nothing seems to me more exact than to go
back to what makes them irremediably different and apparently superior—the availability of tragic destinies. A capacity for destiny, and in particular a tragic destiny. Whereas
we—it would be correct to say that we can't afford the tragic, maybe not even a destiny—our fathers and our mothers
would say We can't afford it. That's why we have aunts in
wheelchairs, who've had a stroke—they watch television,
drooling politely. Meanwhile, in the families of those other people, grandfathers wearing custom-made suits swing
tragically from beams, having hanged themselves because of
financial ruin. So it might happen that a cousin was found
one day with his head bashed in by a blow inflicted from
above, in the setting of a Florentine apartment: the physical
evidence is a Hellenistic statuette representing Temperance.
We, on the other hand, have grandfathers who live forever:
every Sunday, including the one before their death, they go
to the same pastry shop, at the same time, to buy the same
pastries. Our fates are measured, as if the result of a mysterious precept of domestic economy. So, cut off from the tragic,
we receive in inheritance the costume jewels of the drama—
along with the pure gold of fantasy.

This will make us forever lesser, private—and elusive.

But Andre comes from there, and when she looked at
the dark water she saw a river flowing whose sources she had

learned in childhood. As we are beginning to understand, a whole web of deaths weaves hers, and into hers extends the warp of a unique death, generated by the loom of their privileges. So she had climbed up on the iron railing, when we barely managed to lean forward a little, over the black mud. She let herself fall. She must have felt the slap of cold, then the slow sinking.

So we went to the bridge, and were frightened by it. On the way home, on our bicycles, we realized that it was late, and we pedaled hard. We didn't exchange a word. Bobby turned off to his house, then the Saint. Luca and I were left. We rode beside one another, still mute.

I've said that of them all he is my best friend. We can understand each other with a gesture; sometimes just a smile is enough. Before girls arrived, we spent all the afternoons of our lives together—or at least so it seems to us. I know when he's about to leave, and at times I can tell the moment before he starts speaking. I would find him in a crowd, at first glance, just by the way he walks—his shoulders. I seem older than him, we all do, because there's still something of the child about him, in his small bones, his white skin, in the features of his face, which are delicate and very handsome. Like his hands, and his slender neck, and his thin legs. But he doesn't know it, we barely know it—as I said, physical beauty is something we don't pay attention to. It's not necessary for the building of the Kingdom. So Luca wears it without using it—an appointment postponed. Most people find him distant, and girls adore that distance, which they call sadness. But, along with everyone else, he would simply like to be happy.

A couple of years ago, when we were fifteen, we were at my house, on one of those afternoons, lying on the bed reading some Formula 1 magazines—we were in my room. Just next to the bed was a window, and it was open—it overlooked the garden. And in the garden were my parents: they were talking, it was Sunday. We weren't listening, we were reading, but at a certain point we started listening, because my parents had started talking about Luca's mother. They didn't realize that he was there, obviously, and were talking about his mother. They were saying that she was a wonderful woman and it was a pity that she was so unfortunate. They said something about the fact that God had given her a terrible cross to bear. I looked at Luca; he smiled and made a sign to me to sit still, to not make a noise. He seemed amused by the thing. So we went on listening. Outside, in the garden, my mother was saying that it must be something terrible to live with a husband so ill, it must be an agonizing solitude. Then she asked my father if he knew how the treatment was going. My father said they had tried everything but the truth is that one is never really cured of those troubles. You just have to hope, he said, that he doesn't decide to do away with himself, sooner or later. He was talking about Luca's father. I began to be ashamed of what they were saying, I looked again at Luca;

he made a gesture as if to say that he didn't understand, he didn't know what they were talking about. He placed a hand on my leg, he didn't want me to move, to make any noise. He wanted to listen. Outside, in the garden, my father was talking about a thing called depression, which evidently was a sickness, because it had to do with drugs and doctors. At a certain point he said, It must be terrible, for the wife and also for the son. Poor things, my mother said. She was silent for a bit and then she repeated, Poor things, meaning Luca and his mother, because they had to live with that sick man. She said that one could only pray, and that she would. Then my father got up; they both got up and went inside. We instinctively lowered our eyes onto the Formula 1 magazines, we were terrified that the door would open. But it didn't. We heard my parents' footsteps, in the hall, as they went toward the living room. We sat there, immobile, our hearts pounding.

We had to get out of there, and it didn't end well. When we got to the garden, my mother came out to ask when I would be back, and so she saw Luca. Then she said his name, in a kind of greeting, but animated by surprise and dismay—unable to add something, as she would have, on an ordinary day. Luca turned to her and said, Good evening, signora. He said it politely, in the most normal tone there is. We are very good at pretending. We left while my mother was still there, in the doorway, motionless, a magazine in her hand, her index finger holding her place.

For a while as we walked, one beside the other, we said nothing. Entrenched in our thoughts, both of us. When we

had to cross a street, I raised my head, and as I was looking
at the cars go by, I looked at Luca, too, for a moment. His
eyes were red, his head bent.

The fact is that it had never occurred to me that his father was *sick*—and the truth, however strange, is that Luca
hadn't thought anything like that, either: this gives an idea
of how we're made. We have a blind faith in our parents;
what we see at home is the just, well-balanced way of things,
the protocol of what we consider mental health. *We adore* our
parents for that reason—they keep us sheltered from any
anomaly. So the hypothesis doesn't exist that they, first of
all, can be an anomaly—*an illness*. Sick mothers do not exist,
only tired ones. Fathers never fail, at times they are irritable.
A certain unhappiness, which we prefer not to register,
occasionally assumes the form of pathologies that must have
names, but at home we don't say them. Resorting to doctors
is unpleasant and, when it happens, moderated by the choice
of doctor friends, familiars of the household, little more than
confidants. Where the aggression of a psychiatrist might be
useful, we prefer the good-humored friendship of doctors
we've known all our lives.

To us this seems normal.

So, without knowing it, we inherit an incapacity for
tragedy, and a predestination to a lesser form of drama:
because in our houses the reality of evil is not accepted, and
this puts off forever any tragic development by triggering
the long swell of a measured and permanent drama—the
swamp in which we have grown up. It's an absurd habitat,

made up of repressed suffering and daily censorships. But we can't see how absurd, because we're swamp reptiles, and it's the only world we know: the swamp for us is normality. That's why we're able to metabolize incredible doses of unhappiness, mistaking it for the proper course of things: the suspicion does not arise that it hides wounds to be healed, and fractures to be pieced together. Similarly, we are ignorant of what scandal is, because we instinctively accept every possible deviation betrayed by those around us simply as an unexpected supplement to the protocol of normality. So, for example, when, in the darkness of the parish cinema, we felt the priest's hand resting on the inside of our thigh, we weren't angry but quickly deduced that evidently things were like that, priests put their hands there—it wasn't something you needed to mention at home. We were twelve, thirteen. We didn't push the priest's hand away. We took the Eucharist from the same hand, the following Sunday. We were capable of doing that, we are still capable of it—why should we not be capable of mistaking depression for a form of elegance, and unhappiness for an appropriate coloration of life? Luca's father never goes to the stadium, because he can't bear to be in the midst of so many people: it's something we know and interpret as a kind of distinction. We are used to considering him vaguely aristocratic, because of his silence, even when we go to the park. He walks slowly and his laughter comes in bursts, as if he were making a concession. He doesn't drive. As far as we remember, he has never raised his voice. All this seems a manifestation of a superior dignity. Nor are we alerted by the fact that everyone around him displays a particular cheerfulness. The exact word would be *forced*, but it never occurs to us, because it's a *particular* cheerfulness, which we interpret as a form of respect—in fact he's an official at the Ministry. Ultimately we consider him a father like the others, only perhaps more opaque—foreign.

But at night Luca sits beside him on the sofa, in front of the television. His father places a hand on his knee. He says nothing. They say nothing. Every so often the father squeezes his son's knee hard.

What does it mean that it's an illness? Luca asked me that day, as we walked.

I don't know, I don't have the slightest idea, I said. It was the truth.

It seemed pointless to go on talking about it, and for a very long time we didn't mention it again. Until that night, when we were coming home from Andre's bridge, and were alone. In front of my house, with our bikes stopped, one foot on the ground, the other on the pedal. My parents were waiting for me, we always have dinner at seven thirty, I don't know why. I should have gone in, but it was clear that Luca had something to say. He shifted his weight onto the other leg, tilting the bike slightly. Then he said that leaning on the railing of the bridge he had understood a memory—he had remembered something and understood it. He waited a moment to see if I had to go. I stayed. At our house, he said, we eat almost in silence. At your house it's different, also at Bobby's or the Saint's, but we always eat in silence. You can hear all the sounds, the forks on the plates, the water in the glasses. My father, especially, is silent. It's always been like that. Then I remembered that many times my father—I remembered that he often gets up, at a certain point, it often happens that he gets up, without saying anything, before we've finished, he gets up, opens the door to the balcony, and goes out on the balcony, pulling the door closed behind him, and then stands there, leaning on the railing. For years I've seen him do that. Mamma and I take advantage of it—we talk, Mamma jokes, she goes to get a plate, a bottle, asks me a question, like that. Through the window there is my father, back to us, a bit bent, leaning on the railing. For years I haven't thought about it, but tonight, on the bridge, it occurred to me what he goes there to do. I think my father goes there to jump off. Then he doesn't have the courage to do it, but every time he gets up and goes there with that idea.

He raised his eyes, because he wanted to look at me.

It's like Andre, he said.

So Luca was the first of us to cross the border. He didn't do it on purpose—he's not a restless kid or anything. He found himself next to an open window while adults were talking incautiously. And, from a distance, he learned about Andre's dying. They are two indiscretions that damaged his—our—homeland. For the first time one of us pushed beyond the inherited borders, in the suspicion that there are no borders, in reality, no mother house untouched. Timidly he began to walk a no-man's-land where the words *suffering* and *death* have a precise meaning—dictated by Andre and written in our language in the handwriting of our parents. From that land he looks at us, waiting for us to follow.

Since Andre is insoluble, in her family they often cite her grandmother, who is dead now. According to their version of human destiny, the worms are eating her. We know, however, that the Judgment Day is waiting, and the end of time. The grandmother was an artist—you can find her in the encyclopedias. Nothing special, but at sixteen she had crossed the ocean with a great English writer: he dictated and she typed, on a Remington Portable. Letters, or parts of books, stories. In America she discovered photography, now she turns up in encyclopedias as a photographer. She liked to photograph derelicts and iron bridges. She did it well, in black and white. She had Hungarian and Spanish blood in her veins, but she married Andre's grandfather in Switzerland—thus becoming very wealthy. We never saw her. She was known for her beauty. Andre resembles her, they say. Also in character.

At a certain point the grandmother stopped taking photographs—she devoted herself to keeping the family together, becoming its gracious tyrant. Her son suffered from this, her only son, and the woman he married, an Italian model: Andre's parents. They were young and insecure, so the grandmother broke them regularly, because she was old and had an inexplicable power. She lived with them and sat at the head of the table—a servant handed her the plates, saying the name of each course in French. Until she died. The grandfather had departed years earlier, it should be said, to complete the picture. Died, to be precise.

Before Andre, Andre's parents had had twins. A boy and a girl. To the grandmother it had seemed rather vulgar—she was convinced that having twins was something poor people did. In particular she couldn't bear the girl, whose name was Lucia. She couldn't see the use of her. Three years later, Andre's mother became pregnant with Andre. The grandmother said that, obviously, she should have an abortion. But she didn't. And here's exactly what happened next.

The day Andre came out of her mother's womb was an April day—the father was traveling, the twins were at home with the grandmother. The clinic telephoned the house to say that the mother had been admitted to the delivery room; the grandmother said, Good. She made sure that the twins had eaten, then she sat down at the table and had lunch. After coffee she let the Spanish nanny go for a couple of hours and took the twins to the garden: it was sunny, a beautiful spring day. She sat down on a recliner and fell asleep, because it happened that she did that, sometimes, after lunch, and didn't think it necessary to behave differently. Or it simply happened—she fell asleep. The twins played on the lawn. There was a pool with a fountain, a stone pool with red and yellow fish. At the center a jet. The twins approached, to play. They threw things they found in the garden into the pool. Lucia, the girl, at a certain point thought it would be nice to touch the water with her hands, and then her feet, and to play in it. She was three, so it wasn't easy, but she managed it, planting her small feet against the stone and pushing her head over the edge. Her brother was half watching her, half picking up things on the lawn. In the end the child slid into the water, making a faint sound, as of a small amphibious animal—a round creature. The pool wasn't deep, barely two feet, but she was scared by the water, maybe she hit the stone bottom, and this must have dulled the instinct that would have simply, naturally, saved her. So she breathed the dark water, and when she sought the air that she needed to cry, she couldn't find it. She turned slightly, laboriously, pushing on her heels and slapping the water with her hands, but they were small hands, and made a light, silvery sound. Then she was motionless among the yellow and red fish, who didn't understand. The brother came over to look. At that moment Andre emerged from her mother's womb, and did so in suffering, as it is written in the book we believe in.

We know this because it's a story that everyone knows—in Andre's world there is no modesty or shame. That's how they hand down their superiority, and underscore their tragic privilege. This predisposes them to rise inevitably into legend—and in fact numerous variants of this story exist. Some say that it was the Spanish nanny who fell asleep, but it's also said that the child was already dead when she was put in the water. The role of the grandmother is always rather ambiguous, but one has to consider the general inclination to base a narrative on the certainty of an evil character—as she, in some ways, surely was. Also the story of the father traveling seemed to many suspect, apocryphal. Yet on one detail all agree, and that is the fact that Andre's lungs took their first breath at the very instant when those of her sister lost the last, as if through a natural dynamic of communicating vessels—as if by a law of conservation of energy, applied on a family scale. They were two girls, and they exchanged lives.

Andre's mother knew it as soon as she came out of the delivery room. Then they brought her Andre, who was sleeping. She hugged her to her breast, and knew absolutely that the mental operation to which she was called was beyond her—or anyone's strength. So she was wounded forever.

When, years later, the grandmother died, there was a quite spectacular funeral, with people coming from all over the world. Andre's mother went in a red dress, which many recall as short and tight.

Often Andre's father, even today, spiteful or distracted, calls Andre by the name of her dead sister—he calls her Lucy, which was what he called the child when he picked her up.

Andre jumped off the bridge fourteen years after the death of her sister. She didn't do it on her birthday, she did it on an ordinary day. But she breathed the dark water, and it was, in a sense, for the second time.

There are four of us, so we play music together, and we are a band. The Saint, Bobby, Luca, and I. We play in church. We're stars, in our world. There's a priest who's famous for his preaching, and we play at his Mass. The church is always over-flowing—people come from other neighborhoods to hear us. We do Masses that last an hour, but everyone likes it that way.

Naturally we've asked ourselves if we really are good, but there's no way of knowing, because we play a certain kind of music, a specialized genre. Somewhere, in the offices of well-known Catholic publishers, someone composes these songs, and we sing them. There's no possibility that any of them could be, outside of there, good songs—if an ordinary singer-songwriter were to sing one, people would wonder what had happened to him. It's not rock, it's not beat music, it's not folk, it's not anything. It's like altars made from millstones, vestments of burlap, terracotta chalices, red-brick churches: the same church that commissioned frescoes from Rubens and cupolas from Borromini is now afflicted with a vaguely Swedish evangelical aesthetic—verging on Protestant. Stuff that has no more relation to true beauty than an oak bench has or a well-made plow: no relation to the beauty that, meanwhile, men are producing outside of there. And this goes for our music as well—it's beautiful only there, there it's *right*. There would be nothing left if it were fed to the outside world.

Still, it's possible that we really are good—you can't exclude it. Bobby especially insists, he says that we should try playing our own songs and doing it outside the church. The parish theater would work well, he says. In fact he knows that it wouldn't work well at all—we should play in smoky places where people smash things and the girls' breasts slip out of their shirts as they dance. It's there that they'd tear us to pieces. Or go mad for us—there's no way of knowing.

To shake things up, Bobby thought of Andre.

Andre dances—they all do, in that world. Girls dance. Modern dance, not the kind on point. They put on shows, or recitals, every so often, and since our girlfriends sometimes dance, we go. So we've seen Andre dance. In a certain sense it's like church; that is, it's a community cut off from the world, with parents and grandparents—it goes without saying there's a lot of applause. But even that dancing bears no relation to true beauty. Only, occasionally, there's some girl who moves on the stage as if producing a force, as if detaching her body from the ground. We realize this, we who don't understand anything about it. Sometimes it's an ugly girl, with an ugly body—the beauty of the body doesn't seem to be important. It's how they do it that counts.

Bobby thought of Andre because she dances like that.

She dances, she doesn't sing.

Who knows, maybe she sings and we don't know it.

Maybe she sings really badly.

Who cares, have you seen how she is up there?

We circle around the point, but the truth is that she's outside the boundary, she's like no one else our age, and we know that if we have a music then we should look for it outside the boundary—and we'd like her to lead us there. We would never admit it, this is understood.

So Bobby telephoned her—on the third try he got her. He introduced himself with his name and last name, and it meant nothing to her. So he added some detail that seemed useful, like where his father's store was, and that he had red hair. She got it. We wanted to ask if you'd sing with us, we have a band. Andre said something, we knew by the fact that Bobby was silent. No, to tell the truth we only play in church, at the moment. Silence. During Mass, yes. Silence. No, you wouldn't have to sing at Mass, the idea is to have a real band and play in local clubs. Silence. Not the songs for Mass, songs made by us. Silence.

We three were standing around Bobby, and he kept gesturing to us to leave him alone, to let him go ahead. At one point he started laughing, but it was somewhat forced. He talked a little longer, then they said goodbye—Bobby hung up.

She said no, he said. He didn't explain.

We were disappointed, of course, but we also felt a certain euphoria, like people who have achieved something. We were aware that we had talked to her. Now she knew that we existed.

So we were in a good mood when we arrived at Luca's house. It had been my idea. No one ever goes to his house, it doesn't seem that his parents like to have visitors, his father hates disturbance—but maybe our going would mean something to Luca and to his mother. So in the end we were invited to dinner. Usually they eat in the kitchen, at a long narrow table that isn't even a table but a counter: the three of them sit there, one beside the other, facing the wall. White. But for the occasion his mother had set the table in the *sala*, which in our houses is a room that isn't used: it's reserved for special occasions in life, not excluding wakes. Anyway it was there that we ate. Luca's father welcomed us with *true* cheerfulness, and when he sat down at the head of the table, showing us our places, he had the air of a man without conditions, confident in his primacy as a father—as if he were the father of us all, that night.

But when the soup was in the bowls, and he had the spoon in his hand, the Saint joined his hands in front of him and began to say words of thanks—his head bent. He said them aloud. They are beautiful words. Gracious Lord, bless the food that your goodness has given us and those who have prepared it. Let us receive it with joy and simplicity of heart, and help us to give to those who are in need. One by one we bowed our heads and repeated his words. Amen. The Saint has a lovely voice, and ancient features—a faint beard, the only one of us. On his thin, already ascetic face. As we know, he has a fierce, adult force when he prays. So to Luca's father it must have seemed that someone had taken his place—as father. Or it appeared to him that he hadn't been able to do what we wanted of him—and that a boy with the face of a mystic had gone to his aid. So he disappeared. His voice wasn't heard, for the entire dinner. He cleaned his plate, he swallowed. He never laughed.

At the end we all got up to clear. It's something we always do, like good boys, but I did it so that I could go into the kitchen and look at the balcony that Luca had told me about. In fact I could see the railing, and it wasn't hard to imagine his father's back, leaning forward, elbows propped, his gaze on the void.

When we left, it seemed to us that things hadn't gone very well. But I was the only one who knew; Bobby and the Saint had never talked to Luca. So we said only that the man was strange. Everything was strange in that house. We were thinking we would not go back.

That Andre knows about me—that I exist—I learned for certain one afternoon when I was sitting on a sofa, with my girlfriend, under a red blanket. She was touching me; it's our way of having sex. In general our girlfriends believe in the God of the Gospels, as we do, and this means that they'll be virgins when they get married—although no mention is made, in the Gospels, of any such practice. So our way of having sex is to spend hours touching each other as we talk. We never come. Almost never. We males touch as much skin as we can, and every so often we stick our hand under their skirts, but not always. They, on the other hand, touch our sex right away, because we unzip our pants and sometimes take them off. This happens in houses where parents, brothers, sisters are just behind the door, and anyone might enter at any moment. So we do everything in a state of precariousness veined with danger. Often there is only a half-open door between sin and punishment, and so the pleasure of touching each other and the fear of being caught, like desire and remorse, are simultaneous, fused in a single emotion that we call, with splendid precision, sex: we know every nuance of it and appreciate its derivation from the guilt complex, of which it is one of several variants. If someone thinks that's a childish way of looking at things, he has understood nothing. Sex is sin: thinking it innocent is a simplification to which only the unhappy surrender.

However, that day the house was empty, so we were doing things with a certain tranquility, verging on boredom. When the doorbell rang my girlfriend pulled down her shirt and said, It's Andre, she's come to get something—she rose and went to open the door. She seemed to know what would happen. I stayed on the sofa, under the blanket. I pulled up my underpants—my jeans were on the floor, I didn't want to be found putting them on. They both came in talking, my girlfriend got back under the blanket and Andre sat on a little wood-and-straw child's chair: she sat in that perfect way she had of doing unimportant things like sitting on a child's wood-and-straw chair when there were normal chairs everywhere in the room, and even the sofa where we were sitting, which was large. And as she sat down she smiled and said Hi, without introductions or anything. The sublime thing was that she didn't care about the jeans on the floor, the blanket, or what the two of us had obviously been doing under it when she arrived. She simply started talking, a short space from my bare legs, with a composure that seemed a verdict—whatever we were doing under the blanket was normal. It was the first time someone had so quickly forgiven me—with that lightness, that smile.

They were talking about a show, my girlfriend was dancing with her, they were putting on a show. They needed lights, I seemed to understand, lights and a seamless gray cloth runner twelve meters long. I was there but I had nothing to do with it and no one spoke to me. I would have gotten up, to wander away, but I was in my underpants. At some point, my girlfriend, as she was speaking, began caressing my thigh, under the blanket, slowly, it was a clean gesture, not exactly a caress, but a sort of unconscious gesture, intended to keep something going, between a before and an after. It was hard to tell if there was some trick, but anyway she was touching me, and I was pleased with her. In fact they will be virgins when they get married, our girlfriends, but that doesn't mean they're afraid: they're not. She was caressing me, and Andre was there. Every so often, but I couldn't tell if it was by chance, she touched my sex, trapped in my underpants. As she did she went on talking about cloth and seams, without even changing her tone of voice, nothing. Whatever she had in mind, the means was perfect. She touched my hard sex, without turning a hair. I thought how I really had to tell Bobby about this, I couldn't wait to tell him. I was thinking of the words to use when Andre got up: she said that she had to go now and as for the cloth she would ask at the theater, for the lights she would think of something. It seemed they had resolved it, the telephone rang, it was there on the table, my girlfriend answered, it was her mother. She rolled her eyes toward the ceiling, then put a hand over the receiver and said My mother... Andre whispered to her to go ahead, not to worry, she was leaving. They said goodbye and my girlfriend nodded at me—she wanted me to go with Andre and close the door. I pushed the blanket away, got up from the sofa, and followed Andre out, along the hall. Reaching the door, she stopped and turned, waiting for me. I took a few more steps: I had never been so close to Andre in my life, and I had never been alone with her, in a space where the two of us were alone. It was even less space than it was, because I was in my underpants, and in underpants my sex can be seen a mile away. She smiled at me, opened the door, and started to go out. But then she turned, and I saw an expression that until an instant before hadn't been there—those wide-open eyes.

The first sentence that Andre ever said to me was Sorry, but do you have any money?

Yes, some.

Could I borrow it?

I went back to look in the pocket of my jeans. My

girlfriend was still on the phone, I nodded at her to say that everything was OK. I got the money, it wasn't much.

It's not much, I said to Andre, as I held out fifteen thousand lire, in front of the open door, where the fluorescent light of the landing mingled with the warm light of the entrance. Often on our landings there are thorny plants that never see the sun but nevertheless live, and they're kept there for two purposes. The first is to make the landing itself seem refined. The second is to bear witness to a very particular stubbornness with regard to life, a silent heroism from which we are to learn something every time we leave the house. No one ever waters them, apparently.

You're nice, Andre said to me. I'll pay you back.

She grazed my cheek with a kiss. To do it she had to get a little closer, and her purse pressed against my underpants, it was just at that level.

Then she left. As if now she had a kind of fever.

As soon as I saw Bobby I told him all about it, slightly exaggerating the business of the touching under the blanket— it ended up that she had actually given me a hand job. He said then that they had surely planned it, it was all set up, one of those games that Andre played, it was incredible that my girlfriend had gone along, you shouldn't underestimate that girl, he said. I knew it hadn't been quite like that, but this did not keep me from going around for a while like someone who had a girlfriend capable of thinking up such plots and carrying them out. It lasted a while, then it passed. But during that time I was different with her—and she was different with me. Until, at a certain point, we got scared—and everything went back to normal.

That's how Andre passes through, sometimes.

On the other hand, the Saint's mother, wanting to talk about him, got it into her head to talk to us, her son's friends, and so she organized the occasion properly, she really organized it—she wanted to talk to us sometime when the Saint wasn't there. Bobby managed to get out of it, but not me or Luca—we found ourselves there, alone with that mother.

She's a plump woman, who pays attention to how she looks, we've never seen her without makeup or in the wrong shoes. Even there, in her house, she was all done up, gleaming, though in a homey, inoffensive way. She wanted to talk about the Saint. She approached it indirectly, but then she asked us what we knew about that business of the priest— that her son was thinking of becoming a priest when he grew up, or maybe even right away. She said it cheerfully, to let us know that she just wanted to find out a little more, that we shouldn't take it as a dangerous question. I said I didn't know. Luca said he had no idea. So she waited a bit. Then she resumed, in a different tone, more confident, putting things in their place; now, finally, she was an adult talking to a couple of kids. We found ourselves compelled to say what we knew.

The Saint has a way of taking everything incredibly seriously, Luca said.

She nodded her head yes.

Sometimes it's hard to understand him, and he never explains, he doesn't like to explain.

You never talk about it, among yourselves?

Talk about it, no.

And so?

She wanted to know. That mother made us tell her that we prayed, while the Saint burned in prayer; and his legs had a way of kneeling that was like crashing, when we simply changed position—he *fell* to his knees. She wanted to know why her son spent hours with the poor, the sick, the criminal, becoming one of them, until he forgot the prudence of dignity, and the limits of charity. She expected to understand what he did during all that time devoted to books, and if we, too, lowered our heads at every reproof, and were incapable of rebellion, and of tense words. She needed to understand better who all these priests were, the letters they wrote to him, the phone calls. She wanted to know if others laughed at him, and how girls looked at him, if with respect—the distance between him and the world. That woman was asking us if it was possible at our age to think of giving one's life to God, and his priests.

If it was only that, we could answer.

Yes.

And how does it occur to you?

Luca smiled. It's an odd question, he said, because it

seemed that everything around us was directing us to that folly, as if toward a light. How surprising was it to discover now how deep their words had gone—and every lesson since we were children, none unheeded? It should be good news, he said.

Not for me, the woman said. She said that they had also taught us moderation, and in fact had done so before anything else, knowing that they would thus deliver the antidote to any teaching that followed.

But there is no moderation in love, said Luca, in such a way that he almost didn't seem himself. In love or in suffering, he added.

The woman looked at him. Then she looked at me. She must have wondered if they were all blind in the face of our mystery, every father and mother, blinded by our apparent youth. Then she asked if we had ever thought of becoming priests.

No.

And why not?

You mean why the Saint and not us?

Why my son?

Because he wants to be saved, I said, and you know from what. I shouldn't have said it, and yet I did, because that woman had brought us there to hear this precise phrase said, and now I had said it.

There are other ways to be saved, she said, without getting frightened.

Maybe. But that's the best.

You think so?

I know, I said. Priests save themselves, they're compelled to; every moment of their life saves them, because in every moment they're not living, so the catastrophe can't strike.

What catastrophe? she asked. She wouldn't stop.

The one the Saint carries with him, I said.

Luca looked at me. He wanted to know if I would stop.

That terrifying catastrophe, I added, to be sure that she understood clearly.

The woman was staring at me. She was trying to find out what I knew about it, and how well we knew her son. At least as well as she knew him, probably. The dark side of the Saint is on the surface of his actions, in the secret passages that he excavates in the light of the sun; his ruin is transparent, he submits to it without much reserve, anyone who's around can understand that it's a catastrophe, and maybe even what sort.

Do you know where he goes when he disappears? the woman asked, firmly.

Sometimes the Saint disappears, there's no doubt about that. Days and nights, then he returns. We know. We even know something more, but this is our life, too, the woman has nothing to do with it.

We shook our heads no. A grimace, also, to reiterate no, we didn't know where he went.

The woman understood. So she said it in another way. You can't help him? she whispered. It was a prayer rather than a question.

We're with him, we like him, he'll always be with us, Luca said. He doesn't frighten us. We're not afraid.

Then the woman's eyes filled with tears, maybe at the memory of how intransigent and infinite the instinct of friendship can be at our age.

No one said anything else for a while. It could have ended there.

But she must have thought she shouldn't be afraid if we weren't. So, still weeping, but faintly, she said, It's that business of the demons. It's the priests who put it in his head.

We didn't think she would press so far, but she had the courage—because deep down our mothers harbor, unnoticed, an incomparable audacity. They preserve it, dormant, among the prudent gestures of a lifetime, in order to use it fully on what they suspect is the appointed day. They will expend it at the foot of a cross.

The demons are taking him away from me, she said.

In a sense it was true. The way we see it, the story of the demons does come from the priests, but there's also something that has always been part of the Saint, with the power of something innate, and it existed before the priests gave it a name. None of us have that sensitivity to evil, a kind of morbid, terrifying attraction—increasingly morbid, inevitably, because it is terrifying—as none of us have the same vocation as the Saint for goodness, sacrifice, meekness, which are the consequence of that terror. Maybe there would be no need to trouble the demon, but in our world sanctity is closely entwined with an unspeakable familiarity with evil, as the

Gospels testify in the episode of the temptations, and as the murky lives of the mystics tell us. So there is talk of demons, without the prudence that one should have in talking of demons. And in the presence of pure souls like ours—of boys. The priests have no pity in this matter. Or prudence. They eviscerated the Saint with these stories.

What we can do, we do. We give lightness to our time with him, and we follow him everywhere, into the recesses of good, and those of evil—as far as we can, in the former as in the latter. We do it not only out of friendly compassion but also out of true fascination, drawn by what he knows, and accomplishes. Disciples, brothers. In the light of his childish sanctity we learn things, and this is a privilege. When the demons surface, we endure his upward gaze as long as we can. Then we let him go, and wait for him to return. We forget the terror, and are capable of normal days with him, after any yesterday. We don't even think about it much, and if that woman had not compelled us to, we would almost never think about it. In fact I shouldn't even have mentioned it.

The woman told us frightening things that happened at home sometimes, but we had already stopped listening. She had in her heart the burden of so much suffering, and now she was freeing herself of it, by explaining to us what it meant that the demons were taking away her son. It wasn't for us. We started listening again only when we heard the name of Andre, dragged along in the flow of words—a question that irritated us, sounding with pointless clarity, right in the middle.

Why is my son obsessed with that girl?

We were no longer there.

The woman understood.

She set a cake out on the table, still warm, and a bottle of Coke, already opened. She wanted to talk about normal things, and she did so politely. She was so direct, and simple, that it occurred to Luca to tell her about his family, but not the truth—little things, as of a normal, happy family. Maybe he thought that she also knew, and he insisted on telling her that really everything was fine. I don't know.

You're good boys, the Saint's mother said at a certain point.

Naturally we go to school every day. But that's a story of embarrassing humiliation and useless aggravation. It has nothing to do with what we would define as *life*.

When Andre cut her hair like that, all the others did, too. Cut short above the forehead and around the ears. The rest long as before, American Indian style. She did it herself, in front of the mirror.

One followed her, then all the others—the girls who hung around her. Three, four. One day, my girlfriend.

The way they move is different, after that—feral. Their speech is harsh, when they remember, and they have a new pride. What had existed invisibly behind their behavior became visible—that they are all waiting to learn from Andre how to live. Without admitting it—in fact sometimes they despise her. But they succumb—although it seems a game.

Also thinness. Which Andre chose at a certain point, as a natural and definitive premise. It's not worth discussing, clearly it has to be that way. There do not seem to be doctors who can utter the word *malnutrition*—so the bodies slip away without warning or worry, only surprise. They eat when no one sees them. They vomit in secret. Actions that were perfectly simple become obscure, growing complicated as we would never have believed, and as youth should not expect.

There is no sadness in this, but, rather, a metamorphosis that makes them strong. We notice that they carry their bodies differently now, as if they had suddenly become conscious of them, or had accepted ownership. Having been capable of forcing the body, they free themselves of it with a lightness that borders on carelessness. They are beginning to discover how one can abandon it to chance. Place it in someone else's hands, and then get it back.

All this comes from Andre, obviously, but it should also be said that the derivation is almost imperceptible, because in fact they don't talk to each other much, and you never see them in a group, or being physically close—they aren't really friends, no one is a *friend* of Andre. It's a silent contagion, fostered by distance. It's a spell. My girlfriend, for instance, sees Andre because she dances with her, but otherwise she inhabits a different world, and different latitudes. When she happens to utter Andre's name it's in a tone of superiority, as if she knew what kind of makeup she wore, or pitied her fate.

And yet.

She and I have a private game—we write to each other in secrecy. In parallel with what we say and do together, we write, as if we were ourselves but in a second life. Of what we write in those letters—notes—we never speak. Yet there we tell each other truths. Technically we use a system we're proud of—I invented it. We leave the notes in a window at school, a window where no one goes. We stick them between the glass and the aluminum. There's not much chance that someone else might read them, just enough to provide a hint of tension. Besides, we write in block letters, the notes could be anybody's.

Soon after that business of the hair, I found a note that said,

> Last night after dancing we went with Andre to her house, other people were there. I drank a lot, sorry, love. At one point I was lying on her bed. Tell me if you want me to go on.

I do, I answered.

> Andre and someone else pulled up my sweater.

We were laughing. With my eyes closed I felt good, they touched me and kissed me. After a while hands I don't know touched my breasts, I never opened my eyes, it was nice. I felt a hand under my skirt, between my legs, then I got up, I didn't want that. I opened my eyes, there were others on the bed. I didn't want them to touch me between the legs. I love you so much, my love. Forgive me, my love.

We never spoke about it afterward, ever. What is said in the second life doesn't exist in the first—otherwise the game is ruined forever. But I brooded about that story, and so one evening I came out with a sentence that I had been pondering for some time.

Andre killed herself, a while ago, did you know?

She knew.

She will go on killing herself until she's finished, I said to her. I also wanted to talk about food, about the body, about sex.

But she said, Maybe one dies in many ways, and every so often I wonder if we, too, are not dying, without knowing it. She, at least, knows.

We aren't dying, I said.

I'm not sure. Luca is dying.

It's not true.

And the Saint, he is, too.

What do you mean?

I don't know. Sorry.

She said it, but she didn't know, either, it was little more than an intuition, a gleam. We proceed by means of flashes, the rest is darkness. A clear darkness filled with dark light.

In the Gospels there's an episode that we love, along with its name: Emmaus. A few days after the death of Christ, two men are walking on the road that leads to the town of Emmaus, talking about what happened on Calvary, and about some strange rumors, about open graves and empty tombs. A third man approaches and asks what they're talking about. So the two say, What, you don't know anything about what happened in Jerusalem?

What happened? he asks. The two tell him. The death of Christ and everything else. He listens.

When, afterward, he is about to leave, the two say, It's late, stay and eat with us. We can eat together and continue talking.

And he stays with them. During dinner, the man breaks bread, tranquilly, naturally. Then the two men understand and recognize in him the Messiah. He disappears.

Left alone, the two men say to each other, How could we not have known? For all the time he was with us, the Messiah was with us, and we didn't realize it.

We like the linearity—the simplicity of the story. And its realism, without frills. The men's only gestures are elementary, necessary, so that in the end the disappearance of Christ seems taken for granted, like a habit. Linearity pleases us, but it would not be enough to make us love that story so much, which we do love so much but for yet another reason: in the whole story, no one knows. At the beginning Jesus himself seems not to know about himself, and his death. Then the men don't know about him, and his resurrection. At the end they ask themselves, How could we?

We are familiar with that question.

How, for so long, could we know nothing of what was, and yet sit at the table of everything and every person met on the road? Small hearts—we nourish them on grand illusions, and at the end of the process we walk like the disciples in Emmaus, blind, alongside friends and lovers we don't recognize—trusting in a God who no longer knows about himself. For this reason we are acquainted with the beginning of things and later we experience their end, but we always miss their heart. We are dawn and epilogue—forever belated discovery.

Perhaps there is a gesture that will enable us to understand. But for now we're alive, all of us. I explained it to my girlfriend. I want you to know that Andre is dying and we are alive, that's all, there's nothing else to understand for now.

We are also solid, and have a strength illogical for our age. They teach it along with faith, a phenomenon that is indefinable but a hard rock, a diamond. We go through the world with a confidence in which all our timidity dissolves, leading us over the threshold of the ridiculous. Often people have no defense, because we act shamelessly; they simply accept without understanding, disarmed by our candor.

We do crazy things.

One day, we went to see Andre's mother.

It was partly because the Saint had the idea. Since the day of the blow job in the car, and then later, because of other things that happened. I think he had the notion of saving Andre, in some way. The way he knew was to persuade her to talk to a priest.

It was a foolish idea, but then there was that business of the hair, and the note from my girlfriend—the thinness, too. I couldn't keep still about it, and it's typical of the way we act to approach things indirectly and make them a question of salvation or perdition, something grandiose. It didn't even cross our minds that it's all simpler—normal wounds to heal with natural acts, like getting mad or doing despicable things. We don't know about such shortcuts.

So at a certain point it seemed to me reasonable to go. We have childish ideas—if a child is bad, you tell its mother.

I said so to the Saint. We went. We have no sense of the ridiculous. The elect never do.

Andre's mother is a magnificent woman, but with a kind of beauty that we have no attraction or susceptibility to. She was sitting on an enormous sofa, in their house, which is luxurious.

We had seen her other times, just in passing, the luminous wake of an elegant apparition, behind large dark glasses. A designer purse on her arm, which is bent in a V, like

French women in the movies. The hand is lifted, and there it remains, palm facing upward, open, waiting for someone to place a delicate object in it, perhaps a fruit.

From the sofa she looked at us and I can't forget the respect that at first she seemed capable of—she didn't even know who we were, and everything must have seemed surreal. But as I said, life had broken her, and probably it was a long time since she'd been afraid of the absurd creeping into the geometry of good sense. She kept her eyes slightly wide open, maybe because of medications, as if in a deliberate effort not to close them. We were there to tell her that her daughter was lost.

But the Saint has a beautiful voice, like a preacher. However crazy what he had to say, he said it in a way that sounded pure, without a hint of the ridiculous, and with the strength of dignity. Candor is stunning.

The woman listened. She lighted a cigarette with a gilded filter, smoked it halfway down. It wasn't easy to tell what she was thinking, because there was nothing on her face but that effort not to close her eyes. Every so often she crossed her legs, which she wore like a decoration.

The Saint managed to say everything without naming anything, and he never even said *Andre*, but only *your daughter*. So he summed up all we knew, and asked if this was really what the woman wanted for her daughter, to lose herself in sin, in spite of her talents and her marvelousness, because the woman hadn't been able to point out to her the rough road of innocence. For then we really couldn't understand it, and that was why we had come—to tell her.

We were just boys, and, having finished our home-work, had taken the bus to get to that beautiful house, with the precise purpose of explaining to an adult how the way she lived and behaved as a parent was leading to ruin a girl we hardly knew and who would be lost, dragging down with her all the weak souls she met on her path.

She should have thrown us out. We would have liked it. Martyrs.

Instead she asked a question.

What do you think I should do?

To me it was astonishing. But not to the Saint, who was following the thread of his thoughts.

Make her go to church, he said.

She should confess, he added.

He was so frighteningly certain that not even I doubted that it was the right thing to say at that moment. The folly of saints.

Then he told her about us, without arrogance, but with a confidence that was like a blade. He wanted her to know why we believed, and in what. He had to tell her that there was another way of being in the world, and that we believed it was the way, the truth, and the life. He said that without the diz-zying height of heaven there remains only the earth, a small thing. He said that every man carries within himself hope in a higher and more noble meaning of things, and that they had taught us that that hope became certainty in the full light of revelation, and a daily task in the half-light of our lives. So we work for the establishment of the Kingdom, he said, which is not a mysterious mission but the patient construction of a promised land, the unconditional homage to our dreams, and the eternal satisfaction of our every desire.

That's why no marvelous thing must fall in vain, because it's a stone of the Kingdom, you see?

He was talking about the marvelousness of Andre.

A cornerstone, he said.

Then he was silent.

The woman had sat listening without ever changing her pose, only darting a few quick glances at me, but out of politeness, not because she expected me to speak. If she thought anything, she hid it well. Allowing herself to be humiliated like that, and by a boy, besides, seemed to make no impression on her—she had let him have his say, about her daughter. Without betraying resentment, or even boredom. When she opened her mouth her tone was entirely courteous.

You said that she should go to confession, she said.

She seemed to have stayed there, before the whole speech. That made her curious.

Yes, answered the Saint.

And why should she do that?

To make peace with herself. And with God.

Is that why one confesses?

To wipe out our sins and find peace.

Then she said yes, with a nod of her head. As of something that she could understand. Then she got up.

There must have been a way of putting an end to all that, and the simplest was to thank us, close the door behind us, forget. Smile about it, later. But that woman had time, and she must have stopped being compliant long ago. So she stood there, silently, as if on the edge of a farewell, but then she sat down again, in the same exact position as before, but her gaze was different, with a hardness that she had kept in reserve, and she said that she remembered the last time she had confessed, she remembered when she had gone to confession for the last time. It was in a very beautiful church, of pale stone, whose very proportions and symmetry inclined toward peace. It had seemed to her natural then to seek a confessor, although she had no familiarity with the act, and no faith in the sacraments. But it had seemed to her the right thing to do, to complete that unfamiliar beauty. I saw a monk, she told us. White robe, wide sleeves over narrow wrists, pale hands. There was no confessional, the monk was seated, she sat opposite him, she was ashamed of her short dress, but she forgot about it at the first words, which were from the monk. He asked her what was weighing on her soul. She answered without thinking, she said that she was incapable of being grateful to life and this was the greatest of sins. I was calm, she told us, but my voice wanted nothing to do with my calm, it seemed to see an abyss that I couldn't see, so it trembled. I said that that was the first sin and also the last. Everything in my life was wonderful, but I was unable to be grateful, and I was ashamed of my happiness. If it's not happiness, I said to the monk, it's at least joy, or good fortune, granted as it is to few other people, but to me yes, and yet I am never able to translate it into any peace of mind. The monk said nothing, but then he wanted to know if she prayed. He was younger than she was, his head completely shaved, a hint of a foreign accent. I don't pray, I told him, I don't go to church, I would like to tell you about my life, I told him about it, something about it. But I don't repent of this, I said finally. I would like to repent of my unhappiness. It didn't make sense, but I was crying. Then the monk leaned toward me and said I mustn't be afraid. He didn't smile, he wasn't paternal, he was nothing. He was a voice. He said that I mustn't be afraid, and then many other things that I don't remember, I remember the voice. And the gesture at the end. His hands approached my face, and then one touched my forehead and made the sign of the cross. Lightly.

Andre's mother had kept her eyes lowered during the story, staring at the floor. She searched for words. But then she looked at us, for what she still had to say.

I went back the next day to find him. No confession, a long walk. Then I went back again, and again. I couldn't help it. I returned also when he began to ask me to return. It was all very slow. But every time something was consummated. The first time we kissed it was I who wanted it. The rest he wanted. I could have stopped at any moment; I didn't love him so much, I could have done it. But instead I went all the way with him, because it was unusual—it was the spectacle of perdition. I wanted to see up to what point men of God can make love. So I didn't save him. I never found a good reason to save him from me. He killed himself eight years later. He left me a note. I remember only that he spoke of the weight of the cross, but unintelligibly.

She looked at us. She still had something to say and it was just for us.

Andre is his daughter, she said. She knows it.

She made a small, treacherous pause.

I imagine that God knows, too, she added. Because he has not been stingy with punishment.

But it wasn't her look that struck me; it was the Saint's, a look I knew, which had to do with the demons. He is like a blind man at such moments, because he sees everything but somewhere else—within himself. We had to leave. I got up and found the right words to smooth over the sudden rush—it seemed I had gone there just for that reason, that must have been what I knew how to do. Andre's mother was perfect, she even thanked us, without a hint of irony. She shook our hands as she said goodbye. Before we left I caught a glimpse of something—leaning against the wall, in the entrance—that absolutely shouldn't be there, but that undoubtedly was Bobby's bass. He plays the bass in our band—his bass is shiny black, with a decal of Gandhi pasted on it. Now it was there, in Andre's house.

We could come back when we wanted, Andre's mother said.

What the hell is your bass doing at Andre's house? We didn't even wait till the next day to ask. A meeting of the prayer group at the parish church that night gave us the opportunity: we were all there, except Luca, the usual business at home.

Bobby turned red, he really hadn't expected that. He said he was playing with Andre.

You're playing? And what are you playing?

The bass, he said.

He was trying to laugh it off. He's like that.

Don't give us that bullshit, what are you playing with her?

Nothing, it's for a show she's doing.

You play with us, Bobby.

And so?

And so if you start playing with someone else you should tell us.

I would have told you.

When?

At that point it was clear that he was upset.

What the fuck do you want from me? I didn't marry you.

He took a step forward.

Why, instead, don't you tell me what *you* were doing there, and what's it all about, your going to her house?

He was right to ask. I explained. I said the Saint and I had gone to talk to Andre's mother. We wanted to tell her about her daughter, that she should do something, Andre was destroying herself and her friends.

You went to Andre's mother to say those things?

I added that the Saint had explained to her about us, about the Church, and what we thought. He had advised her to take Andre to confession, to talk to a priest.

Andre? To confession?

Yes.

You're nuts—out of your minds.

It was the right thing to do, I said.

The right thing? Do you hear yourself? What can you understand about Andre? That's her mother, she'll know perfectly well what to do.

Not necessarily.

She's a grown-up woman, you're a kid.

It doesn't mean anything.

A kid. Who do you think you are, to go and teach her a lesson?

It's the Lord who speaks, with our voice, said the Saint.

Bobby turned to look at him. But he didn't notice that blind man's gaze. He was too angry. You're not a priest yet, Saint, you're a kid, when you're a priest then you can go back and we'll let you do your preaching.

The Saint jumped on him: he's fiendishly agile, at such moments. They ended up on the ground. They were really giving it to each other. It had happened so quickly that I just stood there watching. They did everything in an illogical silence, concentrated, fists in each other's face. Gripping around the neck. Then the Saint banged his head hard, on the ground, and went limp in Bobby's arms. Both of them were bloody.

So we ended up in the emergency room. They asked us what happened.

We had a fight, Bobby said. A question of girls.

The doctor nodded, he didn't care. He took both of them through a glass door, the Saint on a gurney, Bobby on his feet.

I sat waiting in the corridor, by myself, under a poster for those buses where you go to give blood. I went with my father, as a boy. They were parked in the square. My father took off his jacket and rolled up his shirtsleeve. Evidently he was a hero. At the end they gave him a glass of wine and he let me have a taste. I'm eighteen years old and already happiness has the savor of memory.

Bobby came out with two band-aids on his face, nothing complicated, one hand bandaged. He sat down next to me. It was late. There was no need to say we loved each other, but I gave him a pat, so there could be no mistake.

What are you playing with Andre? I asked.

She dances, I play. She asked me, it's for a performance, of that stuff she does.

What's it like?

I don't know. It has nothing to do with what we do. It has no meaning.

What do you mean?

I mean it has no meaning, what we do signifies nothing, there's no story, or idea, nothing. She dances, I play, it's just that.

He sat thinking. I tried to imagine.

So it's not a good action, he said, it's an action and that's all. It has nothing to do with doing something good.

He said that it had to do with doing something *beautiful*.

He struggled to explain, and I to understand, because we are Catholics, and are not used to distinguishing between aesthetic value and moral value. It's like with sex. They taught us that one makes love in order to communicate, and to share joy. One plays music for the same reason. Pleasure has nothing to do with it, pleasure is a resonance, a reverberation. Beauty is just an accident, necessary only in minimal doses.

Bobby said that *he was ashamed* of playing like that, when he did it at Andre's house, it seemed to him that he was naked, and that had made him think.

You know when we talk about *our* music? he said.

Yes.

That we should decide to play *our* music?

Yes.

Given that there's no purpose, only me playing and her dancing, there's no real reason to do it, except that we want to, that we like doing it. We are the reason. In the end the world isn't better, we haven't convinced anyone, we haven't made anyone understand anything—in the end we're us, as in the beginning, but true. And behind, a wake—something that remains, that's *true*.

He was angry with this thing of the true.

Maybe that's what it is, playing *my* music, he said.

I could no longer follow him.

Put like that, it sounds like colossal nonsense, you know? I said.

It is, he said. But it doesn't matter to Andre, in fact it's like anything that can become emotional irritates her. She wanted the bass precisely because it's the minimum of life. And she dances the same way. Whenever it might become emotional, she stops. She stops a step before.

I looked at him.

Every so often, he said, I do something that seems to me beautiful, strong, and then she turns toward me, without stopping dancing, as if she'd heard a wrong note. She doesn't care if it's beautiful in that way. That's not what she's looking for.

I smiled. Did you sleep with her? I asked.

Bobby started laughing. You shit, he said.

Come on, you slept with her.

You really don't understand a damn thing, do you?

Yes, you slept with her.

He got up. He took a few steps in the corridor. We were alone. He kept walking back and forth until he thought the matter was finished. Luca? he asked.

I called him. He might come, he had problems at home.

He should get away from there.

He's eighteen, you can't leave home at eighteen.

Who said?

Come on...

They're simmering there. Is he coming to the hospital, to the larvae?

Larvae is what we call the sick people in the hospital.

Yes. You're the one who doesn't come anymore.

He sat down. Next week I will.

You said that last week, too.

He nodded his head yes. I don't know, I don't feel like it anymore.

No one feels like it, it's that they're expecting us. Can we leave them shipwrecked in their own pee?

He thought for a while. Why not, he said.

Fuck off.

We laughed.

Then the Saint's parents arrived. They didn't ask too many questions, just how was Bobby, and when the Saint would get out. They had stopped trying to understand a while ago, they confined themselves to waiting for the consequences and putting things back in order, every time. So they had come to tidy up, and seemed intent on doing so politely, without causing disturbance. The father had brought something to read.

At one point Bobby said he was sorry, he hadn't meant to hurt him.

Of course, the Saint's mother said, with a smile. The father looked up from his book and said in a gentle tone something our parents often say. Not at all.

The Saint, however, wasn't really better, in the end. They wanted to keep him there, for observation—the head, you never know. They brought us in to him; his parents seemed worried by his underwear more than anything else.

A change of underwear. That in the details the world is saved is something we believe blindly.

The Saint nodded at Bobby, and he went over. They said something to each other. Then one of those gestures.

I stayed with Bobby to sign the papers for the hospital, for the prescriptions—the Saint's parents had already left. When we went out, Luca was there.

Why didn't you come in?

I hate hospitals.

We went toward the tram, shut up like clams in our coats, breathing in fog. It was late, and in the darkness there was only solitude. We didn't speak until we got to the stop. Because a tram stop at night, in our cold fogs, is perfect. Only the necessary words, no gestures. A glance when needed. We speak like old men. Luca wanted to know and we explained, in that way. I told him about the afternoon at Andre's mother's. In those few words it sounded even more absurd.

You're crazy, he said.

They went to preach to her, Bobby said.

And she? asked Luca.

I told the story of the monk. More or less as we had heard it. Up to the point where Andre was his daughter.

First Luca laughed, then he thought for a moment.

It's not true, he said, finally.

She was bullshitting you, he said.

I thought back to how the woman had said it, in search of some nuance that might explain. But it was like beating your head against a wall, nothing came of it. So there remained that hypothesis of a priest in hostile terrain—a low blow. It was better before, us here, them there, to each its own harvest. It was the type of field where we knew how to play. But now it was a different geometry, it was their wild geometry.

Are you coming to the show? Bobby asked. He meant the thing with him and Andre.

Luca had him explain, then said he'd rather kill himself.

And you? Bobby asked, turning to me.

Yes, I'm coming, keep three tickets for me.

Three?

I have two friends who are interested.

The usual two shits?

Them.

OK, three, then.

Thanks.

The tram's coming, said Luca.

But since they had had that fight, they went together to the mountains, Bobby and the Saint. That's what we do. When something breaks between us, we seek exertion and solitude. That is the spiritual luxury we live in—to save ourselves we choose what in a normal life would be punishment and penalty.

We prefer to seek this exertion and solitude in nature. We favor the mountains, for obvious reasons. There the link between effort and ascent is literal, and the straining of every form toward the height obsessive. As we walk amid the peaks, the silence becomes religious, and the surrounding purity is a promise kept—water, air, earth cleared of insects. Ultimately, if you believe in God, the mountains remain the easiest place to do so. The cold compels us to hide our bodies and fatigue disfigures them: thus our daily effort to censure the body is exalted, and after hours of walking we are reduced to steps and thoughts—the bare minimum needed, they taught us, to be ourselves.

They went to the mountains and didn't want anyone to go with them. A pup tent, a few supplies, not even a book or music. To do without is a thing that helps—there's nothing like poverty to bring you close to the truth. They left because they intended to untangle a knot between them. Two days and they would be back.

I knew where they planned to go. There was an exasperatingly long, stony ascent before the approach to the real summit. Walking on stony ground is a penance—I saw the Saint's hand in it; it was his kind of thing. He wanted a penance. But also the light, probably—the light on stony ground is the true light of the earth. And he also wanted the strange sensation that we know up there, as of some soft thing that's left, unmoving, saved from a spell, the last thing, floating.

With some envy, I watched them leave. We know enough to observe the nuances. Bobby had a strange way of performing the small acts of departure—he always showed up with the wrong shoes, like one who doesn't entirely want to go. I asked if he was sure he wanted to go and he shrugged his shoulders. It didn't seem to matter much to him.

The first night they camped on the edge of the stony ground. They put up the tent when it was dark, and the Saint's backpack, lying on a rock, rolled off. It was slightly open, and the few things for the journey slipped out. But, in the light of the gas lantern, there was also a metallic gleam that Bobby didn't immediately recognize. The Saint went to put the things back in the pack, then returned to the tent.

What are you doing with a gun, Bobby asked, but smiling.

Nothing, said the Saint.

It was partly that, but probably even more the words during the night. In the morning they started to climb among the rocks, without speaking, two strangers. The Saint has an implacable way of walking, climbing steadily, silently. Bobby stayed behind—the wrong shoes didn't help. A wind rose from the east and then rain. The cold was bitter. The Saint walked at an even pace, taking short, regular breaks—he never turned. From behind, at a certain point, Bobby shouted something. The Saint turned. Bobby yelled that he was fed up, he was going back. The Saint shook his head and nodded at him, to tell him to cut it out and keep walking, but Bobby didn't want to hear about it, he was yelling, in the voice of one near tears. Then the Saint descended a few meters, slowly, looking carefully where he put his feet. The rain was falling obliquely, and cold. He got within a few large rocks of Bobby, and asked him in a loud voice what the hell was happening.

Nothing, Bobby answered, it's just that I'm turning back.

The Saint came a little closer, but kept a few meters away. You can't do that, he said. Of course I can do it. In fact, you should, too, let's get out of here, it's a shitty hike.

But it wasn't a hike for the Saint; they aren't hikes for us who believe—there is nothing worse than to call them hikes. They are our liturgical rites. So the Saint felt that something had broken irremediably, and he wasn't wrong. He said to Bobby that he felt sorry for him.

Look at you, you shit fanatic, Bobby answered.

They weren't really shouting, but the wind forced them to talk in loud voices. They stood for a while unmoving, not knowing. Then the Saint turned and started to climb again, without a word. Bobby let him go and then began to yell at him that he was crazy, he thought he was a saint, eh?, but he wasn't, everyone knew very well that he wasn't, and his whores!

The Saint kept climbing, it seemed he wasn't even listening, but at a certain point he stopped. He took off the backpack, set it on the ground, opened it, leaned over to get something, and then stood up with the gun clutched in his right hand. Bobby! he shouted. They were far apart, and there was the wind, so he had to shout. Take it, he cried. And he threw him the gun, so that he would take it.

Bobby let it fall among the rocks. Guns scared him. He watched it ricochet on the hard ground and then roll into a hole. When Bobby turned toward the Saint, he saw him from behind, slowly climbing. For a while he didn't understand, but then it occurred to him that the Saint didn't want to be alone with his gun. And he felt a great tenderness for the Saint, as he watched him growing smaller on the stony ground. But he didn't change his mind; he didn't start climbing again, and knew that it would be like that forever.

He went to get the gun. Although he loathed it, he put it in his backpack, so that it would disappear from there and from every solitary place where the Saint might pass. Then he set off on the return trip.

I know this story because Bobby told it to me, with all the details. He wanted to explain to me that probably everything had already happened before, at the slow pace of geological movement, but in the end it was among the rocks that he understood, suddenly, that it was all over. He referred to something we know well—the imprecise expression we use is losing one's faith. It's our nightmare. At every moment along our path we know that something might happen, similar to a total eclipse—losing our faith.

However much the priests can teach us about this possibility, it's comprehensible only if you go back to the experience of the first apostles. They were only a few, the ones closest to Christ, and the day after Calvary, when their Master was taken down from the cross, they gathered together, distraught. It should be remembered that they felt the most human sorrow for the loss of something dear: but no more. None of them, at that moment, were aware that it was not a friend or a prophet or a teacher who had died—but God. It was something they didn't understand. Evidently it wasn't within their capacity to imagine that that man was *truly* God. So they came together, that day, after Calvary, very simply in memory of a beloved and irreplaceable person who had been lost. But the Holy Spirit came upon them from heaven. Thus, suddenly, the veil was torn, and they understood. They now recognized the God with whom they had walked for years, and you can imagine how every little tile of life at that instant returned to their minds, in a light so dazzling that it flung them open, to their depths and forever. In the New Testament, that opening comes to us in the beautiful metaphor of glossolalia: they were suddenly able to speak all the languages of the world—it was a known phenomenon, and connected to the figure of the seer, the soothsayer. It was the seal of a magical comprehension.

Thus, what the priests teach us is that faith is a gift, which comes from on high and belongs to the world of mystery. For this reason it is fragile, like a vision—and, like a vision, untouchable. It is a supernatural event.

Yet we know that it is not so.

We obey the doctrine of the Church, but we also know a different story, one whose roots go back to the docile land that produced us. From somewhere, and in an invisible way, our unhappy families passed on to us an immutable instinct to believe that life is an immense experience.

The more modest the habit they handed down, the more profound, every day, was their buried call to an ambition without limits—an almost irrational sense of expectation. So from childhood we approached the world with the precise intention of restoring it to greatness. We demand that it be just, noble, steady in reaching toward the best, and unstoppable on the path of creation. This makes us rebels, and different. The world outside appears to us for the most part a humiliating, arid duty, completely inadequate to our hopes. In the lives of those who do not believe we see the routine of the condemned, and in their every single gesture we perceive a parody of the humanity we dream of. Any injustice is an insult to our expectations—every sorrow, spite, meanness, brutality. So is any passage without sense—and every man without hope or nobility. Every petty act. Every moment lost.

So, long before God, we believe in man—and this alone, in the beginning, is faith.

It emerges in us in the form of a battle—we are in opposition, we are different, we are mad. What pleases others disgusts us, and what others despise is precious to us. Needless to say, that energizes us. We grow up with the idea of being heroes, yet of a strange type, which does not derive from the classic typology of the hero—we do not love weapons, or violence, or animal struggle. We are female heroes, because we slip into the brawl bare-handed, strong in our childlike candor and invincible in our attitude of irritating modesty. We crawl among the toothed wheels of the world with our heads high but with the step of the humble—the same revoltingly humble and firm step with which Jesus of Nazareth walked the world for all his public life, establishing, before a religious doctrine, a model of behavior. Invincible, as history has shown.

In the depths of this upside-down epic we find God. It's a natural step, which comes by itself. We believe so much in every creature that it's instinctive to think of a creation—a knowing act that we call by the name of God. Thus our faith is not so much a magical and uncontrollable event as a linear deduction—the extension into infinity of an inherited instinct. Seekers of meaning, we are pushed far, and at the end of the journey is God—the total fullness of meaning. Very simple. If we happen to lose that simplicity, the Gospels help us, because in them our journey from man to God is fixed forever in a definite model, where the rebel son of man coincides with the chosen son of God, the two fused into a single heroic flesh. What might be madness in us is there revelation and destiny fulfilled—perfect ideogram. We get from it a certainty without edges—we call it faith.

To lose it is something that happens. But I use here an imprecise expression, which alludes to faith as enchantment, which has nothing to do with us. I will not *lose* faith, Bobby can't *lose* it. We haven't *found* it, we can't *lose* it. It's something different, not magical at all. What comes to mind is the geometric crumbling of a wall—the instant when one point of the structure gives way and the whole thing collapses. Because the stone wall is solid, but in its heart there is always a weak joint, an insecure support. Over time we have learned exactly *where*—the hidden stone that can betray us. It's at the exact point where we place our every heroism, and every religious sentiment: it's where we reject the world of others, where we despise it, out of instinctive certainty, where we know, with utter clarity, that it's meaningless. Only God is enough for us, things never. But it's not always true, it's not true for always. Sometimes it takes just the elegance of another's gesture, or the gratuitous beauty of a secular word. The sparkle of life, found in the wrong destinies. The nobility of evil, at times. A light filters through that we would not have suspected. The rocklike certainty breaks, and everything crumbles. I've seen it in many, I saw it in Bobby. He told me—there are a lot of true things around us, and we don't see them, they are there, and have meaning, without any need for God.

Give me an example, I said.

You, me, as we truly are, not as we pretend to be.

Give me another.

Andre, and even the people around her.

You think people like that *have a meaning?*

Yes.

Why?

They are real.

We aren't?

No.

He meant that in the absence of meaning the world still turns. And in the acrobatics of existing without coordinates there is a beauty, even a nobility, sometimes, that we don't recognize—like a heroism that we've never thought of, *the heroism of some truth*. If you recognize this as you look at the world, even once, then you are lost—there is now a different battle, for you. Growing up in the certainty of being heroes, we become memorable in other legends. God vanishes, like a childish expedient.

Bobby told me that that rocky slope in the mountains had suddenly seemed to him what remained of a ruined fortress. There was no way to walk up it, he said.

We then saw him slip slowly into the distance, but never with his back turned, his eyes still on us, his friends. You would have said that he would return, after a while. We never thought that we would see him truly disappear. But he left the larvae, at the hospital, and all the rest. He still came to play sometimes in church, then nothing. I did the bass parts on the keyboard. It wasn't the same, but above all our growing up wasn't the same, without him. He had a lightness we didn't.

One day he came back to tell us about his show with Andre, if we really wanted to see it. We said yes, and that changed our lives.

It was in a theater outside the city, an hour by car to a small town of dull streets and houses, surrounded by countryside. Provincial. But with an old-fashioned theater, in the square, with boxes and all—a horseshoe. Maybe there were some people from the place, but mainly it was friends and relatives who had come for the show, as if for a wedding, greeting one another at the entrance. We were apart, because there were a lot of them—those whom Bobby called real, while we were not. They disgusted me again anyway.

Nor did the show seem much better to us. With all good will. But it wasn't something we could understand. Besides Andre, there was Bobby playing, some slides projected onto the background, and three other dancers, who were normal people, or even deformed—bodies devoid of beauty. They didn't dance, unless that was dancing, moving according to rules and a precise plan. Every so often other, recorded sounds and noises mixed with Bobby's bass. Cries, all of a sudden—and in the finale.

Bobby's bass still had the Gandhi decal on it—this pleased me. But it was true that he played differently, not only the notes but the prop for his foot, the curve of his back, and above all his face, which was searching and without embarrassment, as if forgetful of the audience—a private face. You saw there, if you wished, Bobby as he was, since he had stopped being Bobby. We looked at him fascinated. The Saint laughed every so often, but softly, in embarrassment.

Then there was Andre. She was in her movements, completely—a body. What I could understand was that she was looking for some necessity that would put the movements in order, as if she had decided to substitute for chance, or naturalness, a sort of necessity, which would hold them together, one inevitably dictating the next. But then who knows. Another thing you could say is that there was a particular, at times hypnotic intensity wherever she was; we knew it, we had seen it in performances at school, but it's not something you can get used to. It takes you by surprise every time, and so it was then while she was dancing.

I should add that it was just as Bobby had said: it didn't mean anything, there was no story, or message, nothing, only that apparent *necessity*. Yet at a certain point Andre was lying on the floor, on her back, and when she got up she let fall the loose white shirt she was wearing, a snake shedding its skin, and became naked before our eyes. And so was given to us, with nothing in exchange, what we had always thought outside our reach—leaving us bewildered. Naked, Andre moved, and, whatever way we sat in the theater seats, it was suddenly inappropriate, even where we put our hands. I tried to keep my eyes steady in an effort to watch the whole scene, but they sought instead the details of the body, to seize the unexpected gift. There was also the vague sensation that it wouldn't last, and therefore urgency, and disappointment when she approached her shirt. But she left it on the floor and moved away again—she avoided it. I don't know if she knew what she was doing with our eyes. Maybe it didn't matter to her, maybe that wasn't the heart of the thing. But it was for us—it should be noted that I, for example, had seen a naked girl four times in my life I had counted. And she was Andre, not a girl. So we looked at her—and the point was that we got nothing sexual from it, nothing that had to do with desire, as if our gaze were detached from the rest of our body, and this seemed to me a kind of magic, that a body could pose like that, naked, as if it were a pure force, not a naked body. Even when I looked between her legs—and I dared to do it because she allowed me to—there was no sex for a long time, as if it had disappeared, only an unheard-of proximity, unthinkable. And this, I seemed to understand, was the only message, the only story that had been told to me on that stage. That business of the naked body. Before the end, Andre dressed again, but slowly, in a man's suit, down to the tie—something symbolic, I imagine. The blond triangle between her thighs disappeared last, in the dark pants with the crease, and it was during that long act of dressing that coughing could be heard in the hall, as of people returning from a distance—so we were aware of the special silence before.

Afterward we went to the dressing rooms. Bobby seemed happy. He embraced us all.

Good? he asked.

Strange, said Luca. But he had barely finished saying it when he had taken Bobby's head in his hands, and leaned his forehead against his, rubbing it a little—we don't make gestures like that, usually, don't bring in bodies between males, when we yield to tenderness, to emotion.

And the Saint, what does the Saint say? asked Bobby.

The Saint was a step behind. He smiled beautifully, and began to shake his head. You're great, he said, between his teeth.

Come here, you shit, said Bobby, and went to embrace him.

I don't know, it was all strange—we were better.

Andre came over then, she came to us, she had made up her mind to. My friends, said Bobby, vaguely. She halted a step away, nodded yes with her head. She was enveloped in a bathrobe, her feet bare. The band, she said, but without disdain—she was noting something. Bobby introduced me first, then Luca, finally the Saint. She stood looking at the Saint, and he didn't look away. They seemed on the point of saying something, both of them. But someone passing by embraced Andre from behind, it was one of those others, all smiles. He told her how beautiful she had been, took her away. Andre said to us one more thing like, Are you really staying? Then she left.

Staying—that was something Bobby had trapped us into. We didn't dare say no, in that period, and he had invited us to go with him, after the performance, to a house of Andre's, a big country house, to sleep—there was a party, and then a bed to sleep in. We don't go readily to others' houses over-night, we don't like the intimacy with others' things—the smells, the used toothbrushes in the bathroom. We don't even go willingly to parties, which aren't very suitable for our singular form of heroism. But we had said yes—we would surely find a way out, this is what we thought.

But people were streaming toward that house, a few kilometers away, in a procession of cars, many of them sports cars. So we couldn't find a loophole to escape through. A polite loophole. We found ourselves at the party, where we didn't really know how to behave. The Saint silently began to drink, and it seemed to us a good solution. Then it became easier. There were some people we knew. I, for example, ran into a friend of my girlfriend. She asked about her, why she wasn't there: We're not much together anymore, I said. Then let's dance, she said, as if it were a natural consequence, the only one. I pulled Luca along, not the Saint, who was talking intently to an old man with long hair—they kept leaning toward each other to pierce the music, which was very loud. In that music we started to dance. Bobby saw us, and seemed content, as if with a problem solved. I, at every passing song, thought it was the last, but then I kept going—Luca came close and shouted in my ear that we were making people laugh, but he meant to convey the opposite, that we were wonderful, and maybe he was right. I don't know how, but I found myself sitting down at the end, next to the friend of my girlfriend. All sweaty, watching the dancing, beating time with our heads. There was no way to talk, we didn't talk. She turned, put her arms around my neck, and kissed me. She had lovely soft lips, she kissed as if she were thirsty. She kept on for a while, and I liked it. Then she went back to looking at people, maybe holding my hand, I don't remember. I was thinking of that kiss, I didn't even know what it was. She got up and started dancing again.

We went to bed when the drugs began to circulate a little too much: either you took drugs or you were really out of place. So we left, because that was not something for us. We had to look for Bobby, to find out where there was a bed, but he was already pretty far gone with weed. We didn't like seeing him like that, and he didn't like spoiling everything because of it. As if she had understood, Andre appeared and led us off, her tone gentle, her gestures controlled—emerging from who knows where; she hadn't been at the party. She led us to a room in the other part of the house.

At a certain point she said, I know, I also get sick of dancing after a while.

It seemed the beginning of a conversation, and so Luca said that he never danced, but that to tell the truth when he did it seemed to him very cool, and he laughed.

Yes, it is, Andre said, looking at him. Then she added, You don't know it, but you are wonderful, you three. Bobby is, too. She walked away, because it wasn't the beginning of a conversation, it was a thing she wanted to say, and that was all.

Maybe it was that phrase, maybe the alcohol and the dancing, but then, left alone, we went on talking for a while, the three of us, as if continuing something. Luca and I lying in a big bed, the Saint settled on a sofa, on the other side of the room. We were talking as if we had a future before us, just discovered. Also about Bobby, and about how we had to bring him back to us. And many of our stories, especially unconfessable ones, but in a different light, without regrets—we felt capable of anything, which happens to the young. Our ears were buzzing, and when we closed our eyes we felt nauseous—but we went on talking, while through the blinds the light filtered in from the garden, to appear in stripes on the ceiling. We stared at them, still talking, without looking at each other. We asked the Saint where he went when he disappeared. He told us. We had no fear of anything. And Luca talked about his father, to the Saint for the first time, to me stories I didn't know. But we seemed capable of anything, and we uttered words that we seemed to understand. Not once did anyone say God. Often we remained silent for a while, because we weren't in a hurry, and wanted this not to end.

But the Saint was talking when we heard a sound, close by—then the door opening. We stopped talking, pulled the sheet up—the usual modesty. It might have been anyone, but it was Andre. She entered the room and closed the door, she was wearing a white T-shirt and nothing else. She looked around, then got into our bed, between Luca and me, as if it had been understood. She did it all quietly, without saying a word. She rested her head on Luca's chest, stayed there without moving for a while, on one side. One leg over his. Luca at first did nothing, then he began to caress her hair, you could still hear the music from the party, in the distance. Then they moved closer and so I sat up in the bed, with the idea of leaving, the only idea that occurred to me. But Andre turned slightly and said Come here, taking my hand. So I lay down behind her, my heart attached to her back, keeping my legs away slightly, at first, but then getting closer, my sex against her smooth skin, which began to move, slowly. I kissed her on the neck, while she brushed Luca's eyes with her lips, slowly. So I heard Luca's breath, and his half-open mouth, from so close. But where I slid my hands, he withdrew his—we touched Andre without touching each other, immediately in agreement that we would not. While she held us, slowly, always silent and looking at us.

She was the secret—this we had known for some time, and now the secret was there, and only one step was missing. We had never wanted anything else. For that reason we let her guide us, and everything was simple, including the things which never had been, for me. I knew nothing like this, but obscurity had disappeared so completely that already I knew what I would see when, at a certain point, I turned toward the Saint, to see him sitting on the sofa, his feet on the floor, staring at us, without expression—a figure from a Spanish painting. He wasn't moving. He was barely breathing. I should have been frightened, because his gaze was close to the one I knew, but I wasn't. Everything was simple, as I said. He didn't make a sign to me, there was nothing he wanted to tell me. Besides his being there, without lowering his gaze. I thought then that everything was true, if he saw it—true and without guilt, if he was silent.

So I looked again at Andre—lying on her back she pulled Luca and pushed him away, between her open legs. We had trained ourselves for so long to have sex without intercourse that for us the truly exciting things are different, certainly not being male inside female—or the animal movement. But looking someone in the eyes who is making love, that I had never imagined—it seemed to me the greatest intimacy possible, like ultimate possession. So I had the sensation that I was truly carrying away the secret. I stared at Andre's eyes, which looked at me, rocking with Luca's thrusts. I knew what was missing, so I leaned over to kiss her on the mouth, I had never done that, I had wanted to forever—she turned her face, offered me her cheek, placed a hand on my shoulders, to push me slightly away. I continued to kiss her, searching for her mouth—she smiled, continuing to escape. She must have understood that I would never stop, so she slid away from Luca, like a game, she bent over me, took my sex in her mouth, her mouth far from mine, as she wanted. My gaze met Luca's, it was the only time, his hair was sticky on his forehead, and there was nothing to do, it was wonderful. I fell back. I thought that now I would look at Andre while she sucked my sex, I would see her like that, once and for all. But instead I placed my hand in her hair and squeezed my fingers, bending my arm and pulling her head toward me. I knew, somewhere, that if I couldn't kiss her everything would be pointless. She let herself be pulled, smiling, she came within a hairsbreadth of my lips, but she was laughing. She climbed on top of me to keep my shoulders pinned to the bed, she laughed a hairsbreadth from my lips, a game. I took her head from behind, and pushed her toward me, first she stiffened, then she was no longer laughing, then I moved my hips in a way that was new to me, she let me enter inside her, and I surrendered, because it was the first time I had had sex in my life. Not even with our whores, never.

We fell asleep when the morning light was on the blinds, the sofa deserted, the Saint vanished who knows where. We slept for hours. When we woke up Andre wasn't there anymore. We looked at each other for a moment, Luca and I. He said Shit. He said it over and over, beating his head against the pillow.

Not long afterward the news spread that Andre was expecting a baby—the girls said it, as of something that was supposed to happen, and had happened.

Luca was terrorized. It was impossible to reason with him, I talked till I was blue in the face that we didn't know anything, that likely it wasn't true. And then who could say it was really ours, that child. I said it like that, *ours*.

We tried to remember how it had happened. That things had functioned in a certain way we knew, but little more. It seemed to us important to know where we had scattered our seed, a very Biblical expression that the priests use in place of *come*. The problem was that we didn't remember exactly—it might seem odd, but it was so. As I've already had occasion to say, we seldom come, and when we do it's by mistake. We have sex in a different way—so, even with Andre, that didn't seem to us the heart of the matter. Yet we concluded that in fact it was inside her that we had come, *also*—and that also was the only thing that made Luca laugh, but just for an instant.

It could be ours, we understood.

The idea was deadly, there was nothing to say. Scarcely born to the art of being sons, we became fathers, victims of an illogical precipitation of events. Beyond the huge complex of guilt, and a shameful, sexual guilt—how would we ever explain, to mothers, fathers, and at school? It was natural to think of particular circumstances, when we would speak and describe it, the details, the absence of reasons, the silences. The tears. Or our parents would discover it first—every time we came home and, pushing open the door, broke that silence, to apprehend if it was the usual mild sadness, or a void signifying disaster. That wasn't living. And without even pressing ahead to think of the aftermath, a real child, its life, in what house, with what fathers and mothers, what money. We didn't get that far, I never saw that child, even once in imagination, I never got that far in those days.

More secretly, I thought back still further, where I saw us exiled in a landscape that wasn't ours, sucked into that vocation for tragedy that belonged to the wealthy—it was a crack, and I could hear the sound of it. We had pushed on too far, following Andre, and for the first time I thought that we would no longer be capable of finding the way back. Apart from the other fears, this was my real terror, but

I never said it to Luca—the rest of our adventure was enough to freeze him.

We lived it by ourselves, it should also be said, keeping everything hidden inside us. We didn't want to talk to Bobby about it, the Saint had disappeared into a void. We had stopped going to visit the larvae, at Mass we were a duo playing and singing, a punishment. I tried it, talking to the Saint, but he escaped, coldly. I managed to stop him once on the way out of school, and nothing came of it. We understood that he needed time. There was no one else around. No priest for matters of that sort. Thus we were so alone—in that solitude that breeds disasters.

And we were so young.

To talk about it with Andre didn't even cross our minds. Nor would she ever come to us, we knew. So we asked around, without putting emphasis in the words, hands in our pockets. People knew that she was expecting a baby, she had said it, to someone, always denying the name of the father. It seemed a fact. Yet I never really believed it until the day I happened to meet Andre's father on the street—he was at the wheel of a red sports car. We had been introduced at the show, just introduced, oddly he remembered me. He drove up to the sidewalk and stopped where I was. Those were days when, if anyone spoke to us, we feared disaster, Luca and I.

Have you seen Andre? he asked.

I thought he meant had I seen how marvelous she was, up on the stage—or even in general, what a marvel she was, in life. So I answered, Yes.

Where? he asked. I said Everywhere. It sounded rather excessive, to tell the truth. So I added, From a distance.

Andre's father nodded yes, as if to say that he agreed, and had understood. He gave a look around. Maybe he was thinking what a strange type I was. You're a smart kid, he said. And drove off.

Four intersections farther on, where a signal flashed uselessly in the sun, the red sports car was hit by an out-of-control van. The impact was terrible, and Andre's father lost his life.

Then I knew that that child was there, because I recognized the squaring of a circle—the meeting of two geometries. The spell that ruled that family, welding every birth to a death, had been crossed with the protocol of our feelings, which linked every sin to a punishment. The result, by all the evidence, was a prison of steel—I distinctly heard the mechanical sound of the lock.

I didn't talk to Luca about it—he had begun to skip school, he didn't answer the phone. I had to go get him to make him leave the house, sometimes, and it wasn't always enough. Everything was difficult in those hours, the pain of keeping things going. One morning I got the idea of taking him to school, so I went to his house, at seven thirty in the morning. At the entrance I met his father—he already had his hat on, briefcase in hand, he was about to go to the office. He was serious and terse, it was clear that that visit of mine, at an abnormal hour, caused him enormous suffering, but he accepted it, like the arrival of a doctor.

Luca was in his room—he was dressed but was lying on the bed, which was made. I closed the door, maybe I intended to raise my voice. I put his books in his bag—a military knapsack, such as we all have, from the secondhand stores. Don't be an idiot, I said, and get up.

Afterward, as we walked to school, he tried to explain, and to me it even seemed that I found a way of making him see some sense, of dissolving his fear. Yet, at a certain point, he was able to say, with the precision of simple words, retrieved from the depths of his shame, what really was consuming him: *I can't do this to my father.* He was convinced that that man would be wounded to death by it, and he wasn't ready for that horror. Really, that was not something I knew how to respond to. It disarms us, in fact, the inclination to think that our life is, above all, a conclusive fragment of the life of our parents, merely entrusted to our care. As if they had charged us, in a moment of weariness, to hold for a moment that epilogue precious to them—it was expected that we would restore it, sooner or later, intact. They would then put it back in place, creating the roundness of a completed life: theirs. But to our weary fathers, who had trusted us, we return sharp-edged fragments, objects that slipped from our fingers. In the muffled slide of such a failure, we find neither the time to reflect nor the light of a rebellion. Only the immobility of the sin. So our lives will return to us, when already it's too late.

In the end, since Luca wouldn't go, I left him alone to fill the void of those morning hours. I preferred to follow the dictate of things, in an orderly fashion. School, homework, obligations. It was something that helped me. I hadn't much else. Ordinarily, in such situations, I have recourse to confession and, secondarily, penance. Yet I felt no urge toward one or the other, in the conviction that I was no longer entitled to the privilege of the sacraments, perhaps not even to the consolation of a pious expiation. So I had no medicine—apart from respect for habits, only the instinct to pray endured. It gave me relief to do it on my knees, for a very long time, in random churches, at the hour when there is just the occasional shuffling of old ladies, every so often the banging of a door. I was with God, without asking anything.

When the day of Andre's father's funeral arrived, Luca and I decided to go.

Bobby was there, too, the Saint wasn't. But we were on one side of the crowded church, Bobby on the other, and he now dressed differently—he had begun to pay attention. It's not something we do. We had seen big groups of people, but seldom so serious, so restrained. Dark glasses and brief nods. Standing, during the Mass, without knowing the words. We know that type of recitation, it has no true connection with any religious feeling, it has to do with elegance, with the need for ritual. But there is no resurrection in those hearts, nothing. At the sign of peace I shook Luca's hand, with a look. We alone knew how much we needed it—peace.

From a distance we looked carefully at Andre, obviously, but under the jacket nothing was legible, the decisive thinness and nothing else. We didn't know enough to understand if we could deduce anything from it.

Outside the church, we embraced Bobby, and then we had no doubt that we should go and say something to Andre, that it would be only polite. Without admitting it, we expected something, the clarity of a signal that she would know how to give. There were people in line, in the sacristy, we waited until Andre stood a little apart from her mother and brother, we watched her smiling, she was the only one not wearing dark glasses, and very beautiful. We approached slowly, waiting our turn, without taking our eyes off her—now that she was there, I suddenly remembered how I had missed her body every moment since that night. I looked for the same thought in Luca's eyes, but he seemed preoccupied and that was all. Andre greeted an elderly couple, then it was our turn. First Luca—then I held out my hand, she shook it, Thank you for coming, smiling, a kiss on the cheek, nothing else. Maybe a moment more, delaying, but I don't know. She was already thanking someone else.

Andre.

It's not ours, I said to Luca, the church behind us, as we walked home. It's not possible that it's ours.

She would have let us know, I thought. I also thought that in that kiss on the cheek everything had disappeared, like the water that closes over, heedless of the rock lying on the streambed. So I was exhilarated, I had been given back my life. I said it to Luca, anyway. He was listening. But he walked with his head bent. I became suspicious, and asked if Andre had said something to him. He didn't answer, he only tilted his head slightly to one side. I couldn't understand what had happened, so I took him by the arm, roughly: What the hell is the matter? His eyes filled with tears, like that other time, leaving my house. He stopped, trembling.

Let's go back, he said.

To Andre?

Yes.

To do? He was really crying now. It took him a moment to become calm enough to speak.

I can't go on, let me go back there, we have to ask her, that's all, we can't go on like this, it's stupid, I can't go on.

He might even be right—but not there, with all those people, at a funeral. I was embarrassed. I told him.

What do I care about their funeral, he said.

He seemed sure.

I said that I, no, I wouldn't go. If you really want to go, go by yourself.

He nodded his head yes.

But you're doing something stupid, I said.

I left. After a while I turned to look, he was still standing there, passing the back of his hand over his eyes.

When I got home I let some time go by, then I began calling him at his house—they always said he wasn't back yet. I didn't like it, this thing, and I ended up having some ugly thoughts. I thought of going to look for him:

the certainty that I shouldn't have left him alone there, in the middle of the street, increased. Then I imagined that I would find him with Andre, somewhere, and the embarrassment of the gestures, the words to say. It was all complicated. There was no way to distract myself. The only thing I could do was keep calling his house, always apologizing profusely. The sixth time he answered.

Christ, Luca, don't play any more tricks like that.

What's wrong?

Nothing. Did you go?

He was silent for a moment. Then he said no.

No?

I can't explain now, really.

OK, I said. Better that way. It will come out all right. I really believed it. I felt like talking some nonsense, so I began talking about Bobby's shoes at the funeral. You couldn't believe that he had *actually* bought them.

And the shirt? said Luca. They don't even know how to *iron* shirts like that, at my house, he said.

But that night at dinner he got up suddenly, to carry the plates to the sink, and instead of going back to sit at that counter, with the wall in front of him, he went out on the balcony. He leaned against the railing, where he had seen his father a thousand times—but backward, his eyes toward the kitchen. Maybe he looked at everything one more time. Then he fell backward, into the void.

The ambiguous story of the death of Lazarus is told in the Gospel of John, and only there. While Jesus is far away, preaching, he finds out that a friend of his, in Bethany, has fallen gravely ill. Two days pass, and at dawn on the third day Jesus tells his disciples to prepare to return to Judaea. They ask why and he says, Our friend Lazarus has gone to sleep, let us go and wake him. So he starts off, and, arriving at the gates of Bethany, he sees Martha, a sister of Lazarus, running toward him. When she reaches him, she says, Lord, if you had been here, my brother would not be dead. Entering the city, Jesus meets the other sister of Lazarus, Mary. And she says, Lord, if you had been here, my brother would not be dead.

Only I knew why. For the others Luca's death was a mystery—the dubious result of unclear causes. Naturally the long shadow of the illness in that family was known without anyone having to say it: the father. But people were little disposed to admit even that, considering it something nonessential. Youth, rather, seemed the root of the evil—a youth that could no longer be understood.

They sought me out, to understand. They wouldn't really have listened to me—they wanted only to know if there was something hidden, unsaid. Secrets. They were not far from the truth, but they had to do without my help—for days I saw no one. An unfamiliar hardness, and even indifference—that was how I reacted. My parents were worried, the other adults disturbed, the priests. I didn't go to the funeral, there was no resurrection in my heart.

Bobby showed up. The Saint wrote a letter. I didn't open the letter. I wouldn't see Bobby.

I tried to extinguish an image, Luca with his hair stuck to his forehead, in Andre's bed, but that did not leave me, nor would it ever leave me, so that is what I remember of him, forever. We existed in the same love, at that moment— we had been only that, for years. Her beauty, his tears, my strength, his steps, my praying—we were in the same love. His music, my books, my delays, his afternoons alone—we were in the same love. The air in our faces, the cold in our hands, his forgetfulness, my certainty, Andre's body—we were in the same love. So we died together—and until I die we'll live together.

The adults were disturbed above all by our staying apart and not seeking each other out—Bobby, the Saint, and I. They would have liked us to be close, cushioning the blow—they watched us in wonder. In this they read an enduring wound, one deeper than they wanted to imagine. But it was like birds after a gunshot, scattering apart, waiting for the moment to become a flock again—or even only dark stains lined up on the wire. We just brushed against each other a couple of times. We knew the time that had to pass—the silence.

But one day the girl who had been my girlfriend came, and I went out with her. We hadn't seen each other for a while, it was all strange. She was driving a car now, a small old car that her parents had given her when she turned eighteen. She was proud of it, and wanted me to see it. She was dressed nicely, but not like someone who wanted to start up again, or anything like that. Her hair tied back, low-heeled shoes, normal. I went—it was lovely to watch her drive, the gestures still precise, as if she were taking dictation, but meanwhile something like a woman had slipped inside the girl I knew. Maybe it was that. But also the knowledge that she had nothing to do with it, so that telling her would be like drawing on a blank page. So I did. She was the first person in the world to whom I told the whole story—Andre, Luca, and me. She drove, I talked. It wasn't always easy to find the words, she waited and I talked, in the end. She kept her eyes on the windshield and, when necessary, on the rearview mirror, never on me—her hands on the wheel, her back not really relaxed against the seat back. At a certain point the streetlights went on in the city.

She looked at me only at the end, when she stopped at my house, parking head on, a little away from the sidewalk—something my father can't bear. You're crazy, she said. But it didn't have to do with what I had done, it had to do with what I should do. Go to Andre, she said, now, right away, stop being afraid. How can you live without knowing the truth?

In reality we know very well how to live without knowing the truth, always, but I have to admit that on that point she was right, and I said so, and so I was forced to tell her something I had kept to myself—it was hard to tell it. I said that in fact I had tried to see Andre, the truth is that at a certain point I, too, had thought I should, and I had tried. A few days after Luca's death, but more out of resentment than to know—out of revenge. I had gone one evening when I couldn't take it anymore, driven by an unfamiliar spitefulness, and had gone to the bar where it was likely I might find her, among her people. I should have planned the thing much more carefully, but at that moment it seemed I would die if I didn't see her, if I didn't tell her—so, wherever she was I would go there, and that's all. I would *fight* her, it occurred to me. Except that when I got to the street, across from the bar, everyone was outside, holding a glass: I saw her friends from a distance, elegant in their slightly bored lightness of heart. In the midst of them—apart and yet clearly in the midst of them—was the Saint. Leaning against a wall, he, too, holding a glass. Silent, alone, but they passed by and exchanged remarks with him, and smiles. Like animals of the same herd. At one point a girl stopped to talk to him, and meanwhile with her hand she smoothed his hair back— he let her do it.

I didn't even look to see if Andre was there, somewhere. I turned and left quickly—I was just afraid they might see me; nothing else mattered to me. When I got home, I was someone who had given up.

I don't know why, but I saw the Saint there, and nothing else mattered anymore, I told her.

She nodded yes, and then she said, I'm going, and she

started the car. She meant to say that she would go see Andre, and wouldn't hear any objections. I got out without saying much, and saw her go off, with the proper turn signal, and all—politely.

Since I did nothing to stop her, she came back the next day, and had talked to Andre.

She says that she was already pregnant when she made love with you.

In a low voice, again we sat side by side, in the car. But this time under the trees, behind my house.

I thought that Luca had died for nothing.

I also thought of the baby, in Andre's belly, my sex inside her, and those things. What mysterious proximities we are capable of, men and women. And finally I remembered that everything was over and I was no longer a father.

For that reason I did something I never do—I don't cry, I don't know why.

She let me alone, without making a move or saying a word, she clicked the switch for the brights, but softly.

Finally I asked her if Andre had said anything about Luca—if it had at least occurred to her that she had something to do with that flight.

She started laughing, she said.

Laughing?

She said, If that was the problem, he should have come and told me.

I thought that Andre didn't know anything about Luca, and that she had learned nothing about us.

But Andre is right, my girlfriend said, then, Luca can't have killed himself because of that, only you think so.

Why?

Because you're blind.

Meaning?

She shook her head—she didn't want to talk about it.

I moved toward her, as if to kiss her. She placed a hand on my shoulder, holding me away.

Just one kiss, I said to her.

Go, she said.

So I decided to start again. I began to think back, in search of a last solid moment before everything got complicated— the idea was to start from there. I had in mind the steps of the farmer who returns to the fields after the storm. It was just a matter of finding the point where I had left off the sowing, when the first hailstones fell.

I reasoned like that because in moments of confusion we habitually have recourse to an imaginary farmer—even though no one, in our families, ever worked the land, within the memory of man. We come from artisans and merchants, priests and bureaucrats, and yet we have inherited the wisdom of the fields, and made it ours. So we believe in the founding ritual of sowing, and we live trusting in the cyclical nature of everything, summed up by the round of the seasons. From the plow we have learned the ultimate meaning of violence, and from the farmer the trick of patience. Blindly, we believe in the equation between hard work and harvest. It's a sort of symbolic vocabulary—given to us in a mysterious way.

So I thought of starting again, because we know no other instinct, faced with the storms of fate—the stubborn, foolish steps of the farmer.

I had to start to work the land again somewhere, and in the end I decided for the larvae, at the hospital. It was the last solid thing I remembered—the four of us with the larvae. The going into and going out of that hospital. I hadn't been for a long time. You can be sure that there you will find everything the way it was before, it doesn't matter what happened to you while you were absent. Maybe the faces and bodies are different—but the suffering and the oblivion are the same. The sisters don't ask questions, and they always welcome you as a gift. They pass by, busy, and at the same time a refrain sounds that is dear to us—Praise be to Jesus Christ, may he always be praised.

At first it all seemed difficult to me—the actions, the words. They told me about those who had gone, I shook hands with the new. The work was the same, the bags of urine. One of the old men saw me, and at one point he remembered me and started bawling at me in a loud voice, wanting to know where the hell we had gone, I and the others. You stopped coming here, he said, when I went over to him. He protested.

I dragged a chair over to the bed and sat down. The food is disgusting, he said, summing up. He asked if I had brought something. Every so often we offered them something to eat—the first grapes, some chocolate. Even cigarettes, but those the Saint brought, we didn't dare. The sisters knew.

I told him that I didn't have anything for him. Things have been complicated lately, I said, in explanation. They've gone a bit wrong.

He looked at me in wonder. Long ago, these men stopped thinking that things can go wrong for others, too.

What the hell do you mean? he said.

Nothing.

Ah, I see.

He had been a gas station attendant when he was young and everything was going well for him. He had also been the president of a soccer team in his neighborhood, for a certain period. He remembered a three-to-two comeback victory, and a cup won on a penalty shoot-out.

He asked me where the kid with the red hair had gone. He made me laugh, he said.

He was talking about Bobby.

He hasn't been here? I asked.

That kid? And who's ever seen him again? He was the only one who made me laugh.

In fact Bobby knows how to handle them. He teases them the whole time—it's something that puts them in a good mood. For disconnecting the catheter, he's a disaster, but no one seems to mind much. If one of them pees blood, they like it that a boy stares at their prick, admiring, and says Christ, you wanna trade?

He didn't even say goodbye, the old man said, he went away and damned if anyone saw him again around here. Where did you hide him? He was cross about this business of Bobby.

He can't come, I said.

Oh no?

No. He's got problems.

He looked at me as if it were my fault. Like?

I was sitting there, on that metal chair, leaning toward him, elbows placed on my knees. He's on drugs, I said.

What the hell are you saying?

Drugs. You know what that is?

Of course I know.

Bobby's on drugs, that's why he doesn't come anymore.

If I had told him that he should get up immediately and leave, taking all his stuff, including the bag of pee, he would have made the same face.

What the hell are you saying? he repeated.

The truth, I said. He can't come because at this moment he's somewhere or other dissolving a brown powder in a spoon warmed by the flame of a lighter. Then he sucks the liquid into a syringe and binds a rubber cord around his forearm. He sticks the needle in his vein and injects the liquid.

The old man looked at me. I indicated the vein, in the crook of his arm.

While he's throwing away the syringe, the drug courses through his bloodstream. When it reaches his brain Bobby feels the horrible knot dissolve, and other things that I don't know. The effect lasts for a while. If you see him at those moments he talks like a drunk and scarcely understands anything. He says stuff he doesn't believe.

The old man nodded.

After a while the effect wears off, it passes slowly. Then Bobby thinks he ought to stop. But after a while the body asks for that stuff, so he looks for money to buy more. If he doesn't find the money, he begins to feel bad. So bad that you, in this bed, can't even imagine. That's why he can't come here. He barely manages to go to school. I only see him when he needs money. So don't expect him to show up, get over it; no laughs for a while. You understand?

He nodded yes. He had one of those strange faces that seem to have something missing. Like someone who shaves off his mustache on a bet.

Shall we empty this bag? I said, pulling down the covers. I leaned over the usual tube. He began to mutter.

What sort of people are you? he said through his teeth.

I disconnected the small tube from the larger, attentively.

You take drugs, you come here acting like good boys, and then you take drugs, shit. He was muttering, but slowly he was raising his voice. Will you tell me who the hell you think you are?

I had unhooked the bag from the side of the bed. The pee was dark, some blood was deposited on the bottom.

I'm talking to you, who the hell do you think you are? I stood up, with the bag in my hand. We're eighteen years old, I said, and we are everything.

When I was in the other room, emptying the bag in the toilet, I heard him shouting, What the fuck do you mean? you're all drug addicts, that's what you are, you come here and act like good boys but you're drug addicts! He shouted that we could stay home, they didn't want us, drug addicts, there. He took it as a personal insult.

But before I finished and left, I also stopped by a new man, who was very small, who seemed to have fled inside his body, to some place where he perhaps felt safe. When I put everything back in place, the empty, washed-out bag hooked to the side of the bed, I ran a hand over his hair, which was sparse and white—the last. He pulled himself up a bit, opened the drawer of the metal night table, and from a shiny wallet took out five hundred lire. Take it, you're a good boy. I didn't want to take it, but he insisted. He said, Take it, buy something nice. I wouldn't even think of it, of taking it, but then the image came to mind of him making the same gesture to a grandson, a son, I don't know, a boy, it occurred to me that it was a gesture he had made many times, to someone he loved. Whoever it was, he wasn't there. There was only me, there.

Thank you, I said.

Then, leaving, I tried to figure out if that sensation of solidity that I always felt, going down the steps of the hospital, would return, but I didn't have time to figure out anything, because at the foot of the steps I saw Luca's father standing, elegant—he was waiting for me.

I looked for you at home, he said, but they told me you were here.

He held out his hand, I shook it.

He asked if I would take a short walk with him.

I pushing the bicycle, he carrying his briefcase from work. Walking. I had had for some time a lump in my throat, so almost immediately I said I was sorry I hadn't gone to Luca's funeral. He made a gesture in the air, as if to chase away something. He said that I had been right, and that for him it had truly been torture—he couldn't bear it in fact when people "exhibit the proper emotions." They wanted me to say something, he said, but I refused. What is there to say? he added. Then, after a little silence, he told me that the Saint, on the other hand, had said something, he had gone to the microphone and with an unyielding calm had talked about Luca, and about us. What he had said, exactly, Luca's father didn't remember because, he said, he didn't want to get emotional there, in front of everyone, and so he had fixated on certain other thoughts, trying not to listen. But he remembered well that the Saint was magnificent, there at the microphone, that he had an ancient solemnity. At the end he said that Luca had taken every death with him, and what remained for us was the pure gift of living, in the dazzling light of faith. Every death and every fear, Luca's father said, specifying—Luca carried away every death and every fear. That phrase he had heard, and he remembered it clearly.

Strange boy, he said.

I didn't say anything. I was thinking of that time at his house, the business of the prayer at the table.

For a while we went on without words, or speaking of nothing. We had, naturally, to confront that subject of Luca's reasons, and we circled around it a bit. In the end he reached it by the main road—he asked me about Andre.

She's a special girl, isn't she? he asked.

Yes, she is.

She came to the funeral and was kind, he said. Outside, he added, Bobby was sitting on a step, crying. She went to him, took his hand, made him get up, and led him away. It struck me because she walked straight, and walked also for him. I don't know. She seemed like a queen. Is she? he asked.

I smiled. Yes, she's a queen.

He said that it was their way of speaking, when they were young. There were girls who were queens.

Then he asked what there was between her and Luca.

What he knew was that Luca was in love with her. Not that he talked about it, at home, but he had understood from certain things—and then the talk of others, later. He also knew that Andre was expecting a child. He had heard a lot of rumors, during those weeks, and one was that that baby had to do with Luca. But he couldn't say in what sense. He wondered if I could help him understand.

He didn't kill himself because of that, I said.

It wasn't exactly what I thought, but that was what he should think. Besides, he would get there himself.

He waited. He insisted again on knowing if that child could be Luca's, that rumor tormented him.

No, I said. It's not his.

In reality I would have liked to keep him on tenterhooks a bit, but I did it for Luca, I owed it to him, he would not have done that to his father, once for all.

So I said no, it wasn't his.

It was the answer he had come to me for. Something melted in him, then, and for the rest of the walk he was a different man, whom I had never seen. He began telling me about when he and his wife were young. He wanted me to understand that they had been happy. No one wanted them to marry, in their families, but they had very much wanted to, and even though they had given up for a moment, he always knew that they would, and so it was. We both came from terrible families, he said, and the only time that wasn't awful was the time we spent together. He said that there was a lot of moralizing then, but their desire to escape was so strong that right away they began to make love whenever they could, in secret from everyone. Her beauty saved me, a pure beauty, the same as Luca's, he said. Then he must have realized that that type of confession made me uneasy—he broke off. The sexual life of our parents is in fact one of the few things we don't want to know anything about. We like to think it doesn't exist, and never existed. We truly wouldn't know where to put it, in the idea we've formed of them for ourselves. So he switched to talking about the early days of marriage, and of how much they had laughed, in those years. I was no longer really listening. In general these stories are always the same, our parents were all happy when they were young. I expected, rather, to hear when that went wrong, and where the polite wretchedness that we knew instead had begun. I would have liked maybe to know why at a certain point they had gotten *sick*. But he didn't talk about it. Or perhaps he did, but in a way that wasn't clear. I began listening again when in a pleasant tone he told me that his wife was so changed since the death of Luca, it was clear that she blamed him, she hadn't forgiven him. She's drawing it out, he said. Sometimes I come home and she hasn't even made dinner. I'm getting used to opening cans. Frozen food. Frozen minestrone, that's not bad, he said. You should try it. He was acting congenial.

At a certain point he stopped, bent one leg, and placed the briefcase on it, so he could open it. I thought I would bring you these, he said. He took some sheets of paper out of the bag. I think they're songs, written by Luca, we found them among his things. I'm sure he would have wanted to leave them to you.

They really were songs. Or poems, but more likely songs, because there were some chords next to them, in places. But the melody—that Luca had taken away forever.

Thank you, I said.

For what?

When we got to my house, we had to say goodbye. But I had the strange impression that we hadn't said anything.

So, before trying to find a way to say goodbye, I asked if I could ask him something.

Of course, he said. At that point he was so sure of himself.

Once Luca told me that during dinner, at your house, every so often you get up and go out on the balcony. He told me that you stand there, leaning on the railing, looking down. Is that true?

He looked at me in some bewilderment. Maybe, he said. Yes, it's possible.

During dinner, I repeated.

He continued to look at me in bewilderment. Yes, it's possible that I did. Why?

Because I would like to know if when you're there, looking down, it crosses your mind to jump. To kill yourself in that way, I mean.

It was incredible, but he smiled at me. Opening his arms wide. It took him a while to find words.

It's just that it relaxes me to look at things from above, he said, I always did it as a child. We were on the fourth floor, and I'd spend hours at the window watching the cars pass, and stop at the traffic light, and start up again. I don't know why. It's something I like. It's a child's thing.

He spoke in a sympathetic voice, and I even saw in his face something I had never seen, something of the child he had been, a long time ago.

How did you imagine such a thing? he asked, but gently.

Nothing, I said. I was thinking that if there was a truth in that business, not even he knew it anymore. I was thinking that we have no possibility of understanding any-thing, about anything, at any moment. About our parents, our children—maybe nothing.

In saying goodbye, he put his arms around me, with the office briefcase hitting me on the back. I stayed very rigid, in that embrace. So he took a step back and offered me his hand.

I was copying the gesture, but I lacked the farmer's wis-dom—the expert eye that understands the sky and measures its discontent.

After the passing of a time that I don't remember, news appeared in the papers that the body of a transvestite had been found at dawn, outside the city, buried in a hurry, in the gravel of the riverbank. The man had been killed with a gunshot to the back of the neck. The death had occurred forty-eight hours earlier. The transvestite had a name and a last name, which appeared in the article. But it also said that his name was Sylvie. Like Sylvie Vartan.

The news struck me, because we knew Sylvie.

It's hard to remember when—but we started flitting around the whores, at night, on our bicycles. At first they surprised us irresistibly, on the way home from the par-ish youth club, or from a meeting. But then we began to linger, waiting for the time when they showed up on the street corners. Or we'd go back, and pass by again, until they appeared, out of the nothingness—when the life of the city was extinguished. We liked something that we didn't know how to define; certainly, it would never have crossed our minds to pay them—none of us had the money to do it. So it wasn't the idea of going with them that compelled us—what we liked was to pedal to within a few meters and then stand up on the pedal and pass them with the momentum gained, tall on our legs and light in the whirr of coasting. We did it without any caution, in the conviction that we were invisible—in a parallel world that not even we perceived. Sometimes it happened that we'd pass the same street corners during the day, we almost didn't recognize them. It was another city, our nocturnal one.

So we'd pass them by, and often in the end we wouldn't even turn to look. But maybe we'd go back, later, and from the other side of the street, farther away, we'd look at them—the boots, the thighs, those breasts.

They let us. We were like nocturnal butterflies. We appeared now and then.

But one day Bobby stopped right in front, placing one foot on the ground. Give me a kiss? he asked, with that insolent air of his.

She began to laugh. She was the same age as our mothers, and had a different way of living. From that point, we began to be more audacious. Not Luca and I, who follow. But Bobby. And the Saint, in that special way he has—and as if he'd been holding it in reserve for a long time. We'd stand there talking, but quickly, so as not to keep the clients away. We'd contrive to bring a beer, sometimes, to those we'd found congenial. Or sweets. To two in particular, who worked the same corner, on a dark street. They took a liking to us. Theirs was the first house we went to. But to others later. Maybe it's that they'd had enough, on nights without work, and they'd invite us to come up with them. To their small homes, where the bells aren't labeled. Often there were incredible lamps—the radio was always on, even before you went in, as they were putting the key in the lock. You'd walk up the stairs because the residents wouldn't welcome you in the elevator—the only time we were afraid of being discovered was on the stairs and then on the landing. Maybe that's why they often spent a long time looking in their purses for their keys, teasing. They'd take off their heels or boots when they went up the stairs, so as not to make noise.

So we started out as butterflies and then it became something else. It was part of each of us, and we were afraid to think how deeply—while in front of everyone we returned to building the Kingdom, with discipline and purity. We were aware of some rift, between our life and our whores, a secret. No one knew about it and we didn't even report it in confession. We wouldn't have words to explain it. Maybe in the daytime we get from it an echo of shame and disgust, visible in a certain sadness that we carry inside—like imperfect vessels aware of a hidden crack. But we weren't even sure, the division between our life and those nighttime adventures seemed so solid that none of us believed we *really* lived them. Except perhaps the Saint, who in fact stayed in those houses when we left—we didn't want to go home at a time of night that we wouldn't be able to explain. A precaution that he stopped taking, to the point where he started staying out for the whole nights. Days, sometimes. But it was a different thing for him, it was the breath of a vocation, which we didn't have: we stopped at the game. Where for him it was the path of his journey, against the demons.

That was how we knew Sylvie. We didn't like the idea of transvestites, a distortion that we didn't understand, but we soon discovered that they had a particular joy, and a desperation, that made everything simpler—that resulted in an illogical closeness. We had in common this childish expectation of a promised land, and without the least shame we shared the wish to find it. So they write in their bodies that they were everything—the same thing that could be read in our souls.

Further, they displayed a curious strength, based on nothing, and thus like ours. They gave it shape in an insolent beauty, and in the form of light, which you perceived clearly when you arrived on your bicycle at their street corner on a night when they weren't there. So the cars gave a wide berth, and the traffic signal ticked of a time without passion—the shop windows blind, reflecting the darkness. Sylvie knew it, and this was her life, which she explained to us, taking off her heels and putting on the coffee. By day she didn't exist. I never caressed a man's sex, except hers, while she told me how, and Bobby laughed. Without knowing how much to squeeze, until she said that I didn't know how to do it, getting up from the sofa and pulling up her lace panties, then walking, hips swaying, toward the kitchen. She had important clients, and with the money she would bring her brother up from the South—it was the first of her dreams. Then many others, that were different every time she told us—promised lands. Come on over here, she said. Her voice hoarse.

A car was found, a few kilometers upstream, where the river became wider. Stained with blood. Someone had tried to slide it into the water, then had left it there. They traced it to the owner, he said it had been stolen. He was a kid from a good family, whom we had often seen in Andre's circle. He repeated that it had been stolen, then he broke down and began to remember the truth, little by little. He said there were three of them, he and two friends, and they had picked up Sylvie to take her to a party. He was driving, he had stopped at the usual corner, and asked if she wanted to come and have some fun with them. She trusted them, she knew them. So she got in, settling herself on the front seat, and they all went off together. They hadn't taken drugs, and weren't even drunk. They laughed and were happy. At one point the two friends sitting in back took out a gun, and this excited them a little. They passed it around, Sylvie, too, held it—she held it with two fingers and pretended it disgusted her. In the end the other two took it back, and played at shooting people from the window. I read their names in the paper, without emotion, and the Saint's was the first. The only thing I thought, absurdly, was how small

it was written, among all those words—one of many—and
it was his name. At school, where they called him by his
real name, and his last name, I always seemed to see him
stripped naked, even humiliated, because he was the Saint,
as we knew well. So there in the newspaper he was naked,
and in a line with other names—already a prisoner. The boy
sitting next to him, in the car, was another friend of Andre's,
older. Interrogated, he admitted that he was there in the car
that night, but swore it wasn't he who fired the shot. Then
he had helped them bury the body and push the car into
the water. Anyone would have done it, he said, to help his
friends. As for the Saint, the paper reported that he hadn't
said a word since he was arrested at his house—so I knew
that he was still alive, and was still himself. I knew that he
had made use of a precise model of behavior and was apply-
ing it lucidly. From Gethsemane to Calvary, the Master had
established its immutable rules—every lamb can make use
of them in the hour of sacrifice. It's the protocol for a mar-
tyrdom that we, using a term that, if you think about it, is
sublime, call *Passion*—a word that for the rest of the world
means desire. On the basis of careful ballistic tests the police
were able to form a fairly precise idea of events. The one who
had fired had first placed the barrel on Sylvie's neck, then
had pulled the trigger. It didn't seem that it had gone off by
accident. It was ascertained that it was the Saint's gun. No
motive, the papers wrote—boredom.

I cut out the article, I intended to save it. Everything
was complete, I thought—in the infinite shame of the best

of us. The long journey that our lack of movement concealed I saw now in the eyes of everyone, a secret becoming news, and turned into scandal. Like Luca's death, or Bobby's drugs, so the Saint's imprisonment would pass from hand to hand, an incomprehensible object—a plague from on high, without logic, without reason. And yet I knew that it was breath, the long-awaited seed of a perpetual flowering. I couldn't have explained it—it was inscribed in my coldness, which no one could understand. And in every act, which no one could decipher.

The telephone rang all day, that day—at night it rang and it was Andre. She had never called me before. It was the last thing I could have expected. She apologized, she said she would have preferred to see me, but they wouldn't let her out, she was in the clinic, she was about to have the baby. The girl, she corrected herself. She wanted to ask if I knew anything, about that story in the papers.

I was sure that she knew more than I did—it was a strange phone call. I told her I knew very little. And that it was a horrible thing.

But she went on asking—she didn't seem to be much interested in her two friends, it was about the Saint that she was asking. In broken sentences that got lost. She said it couldn't have been him.

But they won't be able to make him say, I said.

She was silent. It's just a stupid thing, she said, he can't be so foolish as to ruin his life for a stupid thing. She was laughing but not convinced.

I thought that only the rich can call a stupid thing a bullet fired deliberately into the head of a human being. Only you can call it a stupid thing, I said.

She was silent for a long time. Maybe, she said. I tried to hang up but she was still there. And finally she said please. Go talk to him, please. Tell him that you talked to me. Tell him that. That you talked to me. Please.

It didn't seem like Andre. The voice was hers, also the tone, but not the words.

I will, I promised. I added something about the baby, that everything would go well.

Yes, she said. We said goodbye.

A kiss, she said. I hung up.

I thought. I was trying to understand what she had *really* been saying. I felt that she hadn't called to ask questions, it wasn't like her, and not to ask a favor, she didn't know how to do it. She had telephoned to tell something to me alone, which she could say to me alone. She had done it as in life she moved, with that elegance, of unnatural supports and rudimentary gestures. She had done it beautifully. I repeated the sentences—I remembered a hidden urgency, in her tone, and the patience of the silences. It was like a design. When I deciphered it, I understood with absolute certainty that the Saint was the father of her baby—something I had always known, but in that way we have of never knowing.

I couldn't do it at first—after a few weeks I went to see the Saint.

As I walked along the corridors that led to the visiting room, my first time in a prison, I had no curiosity about anything, the high ceilings, the bars—all I cared about was talking to him. I thought of the end of all the geography we had imagined for ourselves, the diminishing of distances, the dissolution of any border—us and them. And if we had known how to orient ourselves in that infinite differentness, from the outposts of misfortune where the storm had tossed us. With the thought of asking him, and the certainty that he knew. The rest irritated me and that was all, the procedures, the people. The uniforms, the mean faces.

You came, he said.

Apart from the strange outfit, it was him. A track suit, of the type he never wore. His hair short, but still the monk's beard. A little heavier, it seemed, absurdly.

I had to ask him what had happened—not in the car or with Andre, it wasn't important. What had happened *to us*. I knew, but not with his words, his certainty. I wanted him to remind me why that horror.

It's not a horror, he said.

He asked if I had received his letter. The letter he had sent after Luca's death. I hadn't even opened it, but then later I had. It had made me angry. It wasn't even a letter. There was just the photograph of a painting.

You sent me a Madonna, Saint, what am I to make of a Madonna?

He muttered something, nervously. Then he said that in fact he should have explained to me carefully, but he hadn't had time, in those days too many things were happening. He asked if I had kept it anyway, or what.

What do I know.

Do me a favor, look for it, he said. If you don't find it, I'll send it to you again.

I promised I would look for it.

He seemed relieved. He didn't think he could really explain, without that Madonna. I found it at Andre's, he said, in a book. But I didn't even try to explain to her, he added, you know how she is.

I didn't say anything.

You talked to her? he asked.

Yes.

What does she say?

She doesn't believe it was you. No one believes it.

He made a vague gesture in the air.

I added that Andre was in the clinic when I spoke to her, and she was sorry because she would have liked to visit him, but she couldn't.

He nodded yes.

Do you want me to tell her something?

No, said the Saint. Let it go. He thought for a little. Rather, tell her that I—but then he said nothing. That it's all right like this, he added.

I couldn't swear, but his voice broke slightly, along with a nervous gesture, his hand suddenly raised.

About the child—not even a word.

There was a set time limit for those conversations, and a guard whose job was to make sure it was obeyed. Strange job.

So we began to talk fast—as if pursued. I told him I didn't know where to begin again—and that everything ripped by them I would now mend, but with what thread? I wondered what had survived that sudden acceleration of our slowness, and he understood that I couldn't choose the actions, not remembering anymore which were ours and which theirs. Quickly I told him about the larvae, but also about the silence in the churches, and the pages of the Gospels I had leafed through, looking for the one for myself. I asked him if he ever had doubts that we had dared too much, without having the humility to wait—and if there was a step, in building the Kingdom, that we hadn't understood. I looked in him for a nostalgia that I felt.

Then I said everything in one sentence.

I liked it before—before Andre.

The Saint smiled.

He explained to me then in his most beautiful voice— he's an old man, in that voice. He told me the names, and the geometries.

Every footstep, and the whole road.

Until the guard took a step forward and communicated that it was time—but not meanly. Neutral.

I got up, put the chair back.

We said goodbye, a gesture and something whispered softly.

Then turned away, without looking back.

His certainty stayed in my mind—*it's not a horror.*

What is it, then—I thought.

To get the Madonna in the envelope, the Saint had folded it in four, but neatly, the edges lined up.

It's the page of a book, a big glossy art book. On one side there's just text, on the other the Madonna—with the Child. It's important to say that a single glance can take her in entirely—a letter of the alphabet. Even though the distinct things that figure in the painting are many—mouth, hands, eyes—and two things more distinct than the others: mother and child. But melded in an image that is clearly one, and alone. In the surrounding blackness.

She is a virgin—this should be remembered.

The virginity of the mother of Jesus is a dogma, established by the Council of Constantinople in 553, so it's a matter of faith. In particular, the Catholic Church, hence we, believes that the virginity of Mary is to be considered perpetual—that is, in effect before, during, and after the birth. So this painting portrays a virgin mother and her child.

It should be said that it does so as if an infinite number of virgin mothers of an infinite number of children had been called there, from the far places where they dwelled, to meet in a single possibility, oblivious of negligible differences and singularities—called to a unique existence, of summarizing intensity. Every virgin mother and every child, therefore—this, too, is important. In a sweet gesture of the Madonna, for example, is gathered the whole memory of *every* maternal sweetness—she inclines her head to one side, her temple touches that of the Child, life passes, the blood pulses.

The Child's eyes are closed and his mouth is open—agony, prophecy of death, or simply hunger. The Virgin Mother holds his chin with two fingers—a frame. The Child's swaddling is white, the robe of the Virgin Mother crimson—her veil black, falling over both of them.

The absence of movement is total. There is no weight that must fall, no fold halted in some loosening, no gesture to bring to an end. There is no stopping of time, it's not the gap between a before and an after—it's *always*.

On the face of the Virgin Mother an unseen hand has pushed away every possible expression, leaving a sign that means only itself.

An icon.

If you stare at her for a long time, by degrees your gaze descends, following a path that seems obligatory—like a hypnosis. So every detail comes apart, and in the end the pupil is no longer moving, as it looks, but remains fixed on a single point, where it sees everything—the entire painting and all the worlds assembled in it.

That point is where the eyes are. On the face of the Madonna, the eyes. It was a standard of beauty that they should express nothing. Empty—they do not look, in fact, but are made to receive the look. They are the blind heart of the world. How much mastery is needed to obtain all that. How many errors before reaching that perfection. For generations they passed down the work, without ever losing confidence in knowing how to do it, sooner or later. What urgency drove them, why so much care? What promise were they keeping? What was to be saved, for the sons of the sons, in the work of their hands?

The ambition that we learned—that's what. A secret message, hidden in the back of worship and doctrine. The memory of a *Virgin Mother*. Impossible divinity in whom lay, calmly, all that they knew in human experience as torment and rift. In her they worshipped the idea that in a single beauty every contrary could be reassembled, and all the opposites. They knew that in the sacred one learns this: the hidden unity of extremes, and the capacity we have to call it up in a single perfect gesture—be it a painting or an entire life. Virgin and mother—they came to imagine her as repose, and perfection. They were not appeased until they saw her, produced by their mastery.

So the promise was kept, and the sons of the sons received in inheritance courage and folly. More than any moral inclination, and in a reversal of all the doctrines, what we received from our religious education was a formal model—a model obsessively repeated in the violence of the images that told us the good news. The same mad unity of the Virgin Mother lies in the ecstasy of the martyrs, and in every apocalypse that is the beginning of time, and in the mystery of the demons, who were angels. At its holiest, and most treacherous, it lies in our ultimate and definitive icon, that of Christ nailed to the cross—the reassembling of dizzying extremes, Father Son Holy Ghost, in a single body, which is God and is not him. We have made a fetish of a logical contradiction—we are the only ones who worship a dead god. And then how could we not learn, above all, this capacity for the impossible—and the ambition to close any gap? So, while they were teaching us the straight way, we were already spider webs of paths, and everywhere was our goal.

They did not tell us that it was so difficult. So we draw imperfect Madonnas, surprised not to find at the end those empty eyes—but sorrow and remorse instead. That's why we're wounded, and we die. But it's only a question of patience. Of practice.

The Saint says it's like the fingers of a hand. It's just a matter of closing them slowly, with the force of a gentle grip—even if we had to put there an entire life. He says that we mustn't be frightened, and that if we are everything, that is our beauty, not our sickness. It's the reverse of horror.

He also says that there wasn't a *before Andre*, because we were always like that. Therefore no nostalgia is due us, nor do we have available a way to go back.

He says that nothing happened. Nothing ever happened.

So I returned to the actions I knew, finding them again, one by one. Last, I wanted to go to church, on Sunday, to play. There were other boys by now, a new band—the priest couldn't do without, so he had replaced us. They were young, and didn't have a history, if I can put it like that—there was perhaps one of them, on keyboards, who was any good. The others were boys. Anyway, I asked if I could join, with my guitar, and they were honored. It should be said that when they were thirteen they came to Mass to hear us—so you can understand the situation. One of them even tried, with his hair and beard, to look like the Saint. He was the drummer. Finally I sat there, slightly in the background, with my guitar, and did what I had to do. They wanted me to sing, but I let them understand that no, I wouldn't sing. Being there and playing—nothing else mattered to me.

But I hadn't played two chords of the entrance song when I felt everything rushing at me—how ridiculous my being there was, and how remote any sense of coming home. I was so old, there in the midst—in age, of course, but above all in lost innocence. I was able to hide behind the others; there was only me. The parents, from the pews, and the little brothers looked for me with their eyes, they wanted to see the survivor—and in me the dark shadow of my lost friends. It didn't bother me, I had sought it, maybe I wanted just that, I didn't want anything hidden anymore. It seemed to me that bringing everything to the surface was the first thing to do. So I let myself be looked at—I took it as a humiliation, sincerely there was no narcissism or any form of attention seeking, I experienced it as a humiliation, and to be humiliated like that, without violence, was what I wanted.

At one point the priest managed to mention that I had returned and that the whole community welcomed me, with joyful hearts. Many in the pews nodded yes, and squandered smiles, a happy murmur—all eyes on me. I did nothing. I was only afraid that applause would break out. But it should be said that these are polite people, who know the limits of what is appropriate—an art that is being lost.

Immediately afterward I was staring at the priest's hair, during the sermon, and for the first time realized how it was combed. I should have noticed years ago, but in fact only that day did I really see it. Left long on one side, and combed over the other side of his head, covering the bald spots. So the part, where the hair divided, was ridiculous and low, almost just above the ear. The hair was fair, and combed with the necessary care. Maybe with a gel. Under it, the priest was talking about the mystery of the Immaculate Conception.

Nobody knows this, but the Immaculate Conception has nothing to do with the virginity of Mary. It means that Mary conceived without original sin. Sex has nothing to do with it. And I wondered what importance your hair could have, if you live with the prospect of eternal life, and the building of the Kingdom. How was it possible to waste time on things like that—he must have used a kind of hair spray, he must have gone out one day to *buy it*.

Because I hadn't even learned mercy, or the talent of understanding, from our experiences. Pity for what we are, all of us.

I took advantage of the sermon—that priest was hypnotizing them, I began watching the faces, in the pews, now that they were no longer staring at me. So many people I hadn't seen for a long time. Then, in one of the back pews, first I thought I was mistaken, but it really was her, Andre, sitting in the last seat next to the aisle—she was listening, but looking around, curious.

Maybe it wasn't even the first time she had come.

I hated her now, because I continued to think that she was at the origin of many of our troubles, but undoubtedly at that moment I felt only that in the midst of so many strangers there was someone from my land, so far had the boundaries of my feeling shifted. However absurd, it seemed to me that on that strange raft there was also, then, one of my people—and the instinct to stay close.

But it was a moment.

So, when the Mass was over, I gave her time to leave. I said goodbye to the boys and went to the first pew, knelt down, and prayed, my face in my hands, elbows resting on the wood. It was something I had done often, before. I liked hearing the sounds of the people draining away, yet without seeing them. And finding a point inside myself.

I got up, finally, the velvety movements of the altar boys who were tidying the altar remained.

I turned and Andre was still there, sitting in her place—

the church almost empty. I understood then that the story wasn't over.

I made the sign of the cross and began to go down the aisle between the pews, my back to the altar. Reaching Andre, I stopped and greeted her. She moved over a little on the bench, leaving me room. I sat beside her.

Yet I was brought up to an obstinate resistance, which considers life a noble obligation, to discharge in dignity and fullness. They gave me strength and character, for this, and the legacy of their every sadness, so that I would store it up. Thus it's clear to me that I will never die—except in fleeting acts and forgettable moments. Nor do I doubt that my going will be revealed as sharper than any fear.

And so it will be.

ALESSANDRO BARICCO is a writer, director, and performer. He has won the Prix Médicis Étranger in France and the Selezione Campiello, Viareggio, and Palazzo al Bosco prizes in Italy.

ANN GOLDSTEIN is an editor at the *New Yorker*. She has translated works by Primo Levi, Pier Paolo Pasolini, Alessandro Baricco, Elena Ferrante, among others, and is currently editing the Complete Works of Primo Levi in English. She has been the recipient of several prizes, including a Guggenheim Fellowship, the PEN Renato Poggioli prize, and an award from the Italian Ministry of Foreign Affairs.